A LOVE SONG FOR LUCIFER

A Romance Novel

Willa Lively

WILLA'S LIVELY UPDATES:

New releases, fun bonuses, and news about discounts are available when you sign up for Willa's newsletter.

Sign up here: https: bit.ly/33lEr4i

TABLE OF CONTENTS

CHAPTER ONE
Melody

When I was 10, my fifth-grade teacher reached a conclusion that would change the course of my life. Mrs. Brown asked my dad to come to her classroom and as we sat down, she leaned across her desk and spoke to him as if I wasn't there.

"Melody has trouble expressing her emotions," her plum-lined lips announced every syllable with clarity. My 10-year-old stomach sank at the word 'trouble', the one thing I tried to avoid at all costs.

I remember little else Mrs. Brown said that day, but by the time we left, my dad got the picture that I wasn't exactly *Miss Popular*. When we got into the car, he told me we needed to make a stop. I assumed this meant that I was about to be shipped off to wherever it is all the bad kids go.

Except I wasn't.

Instead, we stopped at a music store and I learned that this "trouble" that Mrs. Brown was so worried about earned me a new guitar and lessons.

And my guitar and I have been getting in to trouble together ever since.

"You want emotion, Mrs. Brown? Fine, I'll give you emotion," I say into my glass of whiskey as a full-grown 26-year-old woman.

"I'm sorry, what was that?" Ryan, the bartender at Bowie's, asks. Well, it's not fair to only call him a bartender as he's become a close friend at this point, which has more to do with the fact that the bar is under my apartment than the other fact that I confide in glasses of whiskey… I think.

"Or was whatever you just said actually meant for the whiskey glass?" Ryan continues.

"I actually meant it for the whiskey glass," I say, glaring up at him defensively. This glass is all I've got tonight. Ryan is busy working and I don't want to bother any of my other friends. It's a Thursday night and they've got actual work tomorrow because, unlike me, they were smart enough to not design their entire lives around a childhood fantasy.

I perk up and move my face from my whiskey to Ryan. "But now that you've joined the conversation, I'm going to play a song while the band is on break, 'kay?"

Before he can answer, I am bee-lining to the stage. It's not like Ryan can complain, they usually pay me to play here and now the only cost is the crowd letting me unleash my anger on them.

"Good evening, ladies and gents," I say with a stone-cold grimace that likely gives away the fact that it is not in fact a good evening. "Just here to play one song, not here to stop the *adiaphorous* performance we're being graced with tonight."

Holy crap, I can't believe I just used that word in a sentence. I've been trying to use 'adiaphorous' for almost a month since it came up in a crossword. And I'm fully aware that I sound like an obnoxious jerk using it, but I am an obnoxious jerk right now. I wonder if the band knows what it means? I certainly didn't and had to solve every other damn clue around it.

I look at the band to check on their reaction, especially the lead singer who takes every opportunity to mansplain music to me when we run into each other here. But they are sipping their beers and looking neither happy nor angry. *Good*, I want to tell them. Showing the word's definition rather than saying it. Mrs. Brown would be so proud.

Ah, Mrs. Brown, the reason I'm here. The anger rushes back into me and this time I know where to put it.

I strum the electric guitar left by the band on the stage and arrange myself near their base drum so I can use it when the time comes. I let the song absorb me. There is nothing adiaphorous about this version of "Seven Nation Army", by the White Stripes. Nope, this is pure rage.

I'm raging at the moment I fell in love with music and decided it would be all I could ever pursue in this life. I'm raging at the band playing here tonight, acting like they're above playing their music in a bar. But most of all, I'm raging at the devil himself, Mr. De la Roche. The man who signed me for a record contract and made me think my whole life was going to be okay, that I could finally *breathe*, only to rip it out from under me a few days later and shatter all the hope that I had so carelessly let grow.

And the song feels good for a little while. The emotion comes out in my breath, in my stomping, in the bite of the metal strings on my fingers. But when I sing the second to last verse, I know this temporary release is ending and I'll still be holding onto nothing but anger and hopelessness when it's all done.

I gaze into the crowd, desperate for someone to demand I keep going so I don't have to face myself. And while many are dancing and clapping along, none of them are looking at me like they understand I *need* this.

That's when I spot two eyes on me. It's the eyes I notice first, even before his decadent good looks. I notice those eyes because I see something familiar in them. Something that tells me we're running on the same fuel in this moment. This emotion I'm putting out matches his and I feel that he *needs* this too. So I look down at the guitar and I give it my all for the close of the song, for him and for me and for anyone else who has ever been made to feel like nothing.

CHAPTER TWO
Lucien

"Really, Cole? Live music?" I glare at my friend Cole, who has dragged me to no-man's-land Brooklyn. Why couldn't we get a scotch in the West Village instead? Unknown live music is the worst type of activity for a night out. Best-case scenario, we spend our valuable free time wasting energy pretending to like it. Worst-case scenario, I get recognized and young hopefuls mob me with links to their social media.

And after the day I've had, I'm not up for terrible music nor being mobbed.

"Relax, man. This place always books great talent. We'll leave if your delicate ears can't handle it."

I grit my teeth and follow him into the grungy bar. Cole is a talent booker, so I get why he wants to come here. But he doesn't come with me to my work, so why should I join him for his?

I'm taken by surprise though when, as soon as we step inside, the energy radiating through the place is palpable. I try to get my bearings to understand what's happening and quickly realize the excitement is being directed in one direction, toward the stage. This isn't the usual vibe of a subpar hipster band forcing the bar to listen to them.

And when I get a full view of the stage, I immediately understand why.

Under the spotlight is a lone performer. She is stomping on a bass drum and singing "Seven Nation Army" by the White Stripes.

Except, she's not only singing it, she's preaching it with anger and fury. It's a song I've heard a million times, yet the words sound visceral and new from her lungs.

She stops stomping on the drum and glares into the crowd, readying for the next line. She's striking, with her sharp and determined gaze peering out from under long pink waves of hair. My spine stiffens when her eyes meet mine for just for a second.

She's reaching the end of the song and practically howls the lyrics at the crowd then goes back to maniacally stomping. Her light pink hair is flying everywhere and the muscles in her long legs tighten with every movement.

Now the entire bar is clapping along with her. Yet she seems lost in her own world.

Cole looks back at me with a self-satisfied expression. "See, man. Quality. I'll get a table and you grab the drinks."

I nod but turn my head back to the stage as I head to the bar, not wanting to miss another second of the song. It's hard to tear my eyes away from something so wild.

She finishes the song and the bar uproars in applause. Yet, this musical maniac barely seems to notice. She throws a hand up and whispers a "thank you" into the microphone, bows her head down and heads off the stage. My eyes stay on her as she glides right to the stretch of bar open next to me, where a lone whiskey glass is waiting for her.

I hate that I'm still looking at her. I'm the one who usually has to dodge eye contact from people staring at me, and this role reversal makes me feel foolish. Yet, I can't look away. A muscle on her jaw is flexed from gritted teeth and I trace it up to her high cheekbones. My gaze keeps going, to her eyes, which are staring into her amber glass. She looks completely unfazed that everyone in the bar is still watching her, including me.

"Bad day?" I say before I can stop myself. Now I'm not only gawking at her, but I'm the guy who talks to girls they don't know, like I think I deserve a perfect stranger's attention. I cringe at myself.

But I *have* had a shit day, and I saw myself in her when she was up there. The raw fury and the passion was like she was speaking a language that I didn't realize people other than me knew.

She looks up, seemingly surprised that there is anyone else in the room. She has bright blue eyes that are jarring up close. Her flushed cheeks and pink hair make them appear other-worldly.

"That obvious?" She says with a wince.

I nod solemnly.

She's the one taking me in now, her eyes tracing my face. "You don't look too thrilled about life either, ya know."

I don't want to be the one to break it to her that I am never thrilled about life, but she's right that I especially am not today.

The bartender, a young thin man with black hair, skips me and goes straight to the singer, who is already bringing her body up and over the bar to give him a kiss on the cheek. "Thanks," little Miss Angry Pink Hair says before she settles her feet back firmly on the ground. Why would she be thanking him? I think the whole bar needs to be thanking her. "Now can I get three picklebacks, pleeeeassee? One for you, one for me, and one for this grumpy man to my right."

The bartender looks at me as if noticing me for the first time. "Oh, okay," he says, seemingly displeased by my inclusion, which I can't argue with him about because what the hell is a pickleback?

Well, it turns out picklebacks are absolutely disgusting and absolutely delicious. They're a shot of whiskey followed by a shot of pickle juice. A perfectly hideous and beautiful creation that at least distracts me from the day I've had.

I order another round immediately.

"Lucien," I say as a extend my hand toward her. "But with your American tongue, Luc is okay, too."

She grimaces at me but extends her hand. "Mel to my friends, but with your stuck-up attitude you can address me by my full name, Melody."

Fair enough.

"What's got you so mad then, *Mel*?" I say, smirking at her. Why do I want to make this already angry little person even angrier?

She throws down the shot, not bothering to wait for me.

"Well, Lucifer. Oh, I'm sorry, *Lucien*," she says in a pretty okay French accent while glaring at me for extra effect. "Like my name, I reserve that kind of intimacy for my friends. And you certainly are not my friend."

"Well, *Mel*, if you're willing to let me buy you a few more of these disgustingly delicious shots then maybe you'll make an exception."

"I'll buy my own shots, Lucifer." Melody looks at her phone, before looking back up at me. "But if you want to drown your sorrows next to me, I'll put up with it until you become more of an asshole than you already are. Only because that sexy French thing you have going is doing good things for my serotonin levels."

I grin. Nobody dares speak to me like this. I wonder if she would treat me any differently if she knew who I am. Who am I kidding? She's a musician. Of course she would treat me differently. I'm like a walking, talking, golden ticket.

Since I'm in a sadistic mood, I'll do whatever it takes for her to *not* find out, just so she will insult me with that tongue of hers some more.

"You taking any requests?" I ask her as the bartender pours us another round.

"One… I'm not a monkey and two, I'm done for the night. Actually, I wasn't even supposed to play tonight, but the band was gracious enough to let me have a cameo," she says avoiding my eyes.

I can tell by her tone that I'm getting close to a sore spot, possibly the reason for her bad mood. She seems to have shutdown from my question. We sit in silence for a little while and I ignore the fact that Cole is probably wondering where the hell I am. For some reason, I'm not quite ready to leave this strange, angry little person. So, to prevent her from avoiding me all together, I open my big mouth.

"My girlfriend of two years dumped me today, an hour before announcing her engagement to an 87-year-old man," I announce a bit too loudly. Even the bartender looks at me with something other than disdain at this announcement. Not the result I intended, but at least Melody has her full attention back on me.

"Dude," the bartender says sympathetically. Rather than completing that sentence, he pours me another round of shots wordlessly.

I glance back at Melody who is not only staring at me, but also has a distorted look on her face…

"Are you holding back a laugh?" I accuse her once I register what is actually happening.

She realizes she's caught and spits out laughter. Literally, the mist from her outburst makes it to my face. She's covering her mouth and I can tell she is trying to stop herself, but she is now practically doubled over in hysterics.

"I'm so glad my misery can provide you so much joy," I say, stifling a smile. To be honest, it's not the biggest reason I'm miserable, but it's the only one I can actually talk about. It's also a perfect example of why I'm fed up with this stupid world that I'm a part of. A world where a 30-year-old billionaire isn't enough, because a girl can have an elderly billionaire who can die quicker.

I was never actually in love with Steph, my now ex-girlfriend. It was convenient, and she was willing to play all the parts I needed her to in my demanding life. Yet, that doesn't mean that it's not going to be hell tomorrow when it's plastered all over every gossip website.

I take the shot without Melody and turn back to her with a cocked eyebrow as she tries to collect herself.

"I am," her face scrunches up as she tries to compose herself. "Oh crap, I am so, so sorry. I don't know what came over me. I've been in such a miserable mood all day and then you come out with something like…that." She takes a deep breath.

"It's just," she continues with the slightest bit more composure. "It's the most ridiculous thing I've ever heard. I didn't think that happens in real life."

I sigh. I can't believe I even told her. I was so eager to change the subject I ended up revealing the most embarrassing thing about me. I kind of emasculated myself on my very first night of being single with the hottest girl I've let myself flirt with in a long time.

Actually, fuck that. It's literally impossible to emasculate me.

"The relationship was a sham, so I don't blame her," I say, playing this move to protect my ego like it's the king on the chessboard.

"Oh yeah, and I'm sure her new relationship is true love," Melody answers with a smile.

"She gambled for the certainty that she'll have her own money, rather than risk it all in the hope of possibly finding love one day. Then, even if she were to find this mythical love that people write and sing about, who's to say that it will be better than being a widowed billionaire? Some might say she made the practical choice," I offer.

I expect Melody to roll her eyes at my cynicism, but she doesn't. Instead, she is looking at me with studious eyes. Some of the melancholy that I saw in her before comes back.

"What do you say?" she finally asks.

"I say that I'm happy for her," I bring my next shot to cheers with Melody, "she certainly wasn't getting either my love or my money, so good riddance."

"You're kind of soulless," Melody says with an expression of both repulsion and attraction. *There we go.* That's the kind of reaction that is in my comfort zone.

"Oh, Mel. You have no idea," I say flatly before throwing more cheap whiskey down my throat.

CHAPTER THREE
Melody

"This is really where you live?" Lucien's figure is hulking when we're not sitting on barstools. And I'm a little drunk, but is it possible that he's the most gorgeous man I've ever seen? No, of course it can't be possible. Yet, when I look at him, it's like I get a hit of dopamine every time. His face is actually *pleasurable* to observe. The curved lips set under a regal nose, and those dark eyes that I spotted from the stage. One of his symmetrical, dark eyebrows cocks at me. I seemed to have stopped working my keys in the door in order to stare at him.

"Listen, Mel," those lips start, "you don't have to pretend to live here. I mean, who in their right mind would choose a place next to a bar. We can go back to my place."

I almost forgot that for the amount of pleasure that his face produces in me, those lips seem to form an equal amount of annoyance when they're actually used for speaking.

"Remind me, why am I letting Lucifer himself into my apartment?" I say as I finally get the key to jiggle just the right amount to unlock my door.

He looks at the door as if impressed that I actually have a home.

"We're going to make beautiful music together, of course." He says with a glimmer in his eye that lights my insides on fire.

Of course I remember why we're here, but I need any excuse to remind him I think he's the devil. And maybe to remind myself.

"This better be one hell of a performance," I say.

He told me at the bar that he can play the guitar and I didn't believe him, so after the band refused to let him use their guitar, I told him that my apartment next door has plenty of instruments that he could prove himself with. The friend Lucien had come with was busy making out with Ryan after he got off his shift, so he agreed. I'm not sure what it is about this infuriating man that makes me not want to part with him. I chalk it up to him being the perfect distraction from a shitty day.

We make it up to my apartment and through the door, which goes straight into my living room. I see his eyes scanning over the space. My apartment is tiny and not luxurious by any standard, but I love it. I'm pretty sure Lucien is the type of wealthy that has never even stepped in an apartment this small. But it's also always hard to tell in New York. He could pour all of his money into the appearance of looking rich, but crawls back to an apartment he shares with 5 other guys two hours away from Manhattan. I don't really care either way about his money situation. He could be as poor as me, but if he spends all his money on stupid expensive things instead of experiencing life, that would be the true turn off, not his bank account.

But I have to admit, I do like the fact that he dresses differently than the guys I usually see hanging around after my shows. No ironic t-shirt, or wearing a beanie inside. Nope. Lucien looks nothing short of elegant in his tailored pants, dress shoes, and dress shirt with rolled-up sleeves that expose his muscled tan arms and a light cast of dark hair. I wonder what he thinks of me, in my thrift-store 80s leather skirt that is completely inappropriate for this

December weather but fine for angrily walking the 3 feet to Bowie's from my apartment.

He walks up close to my wall of instruments to inspect them and then looks back to me, as if I am a stranger who just walked into the room. The expression on his face is curious, as if he is taking me in all over again.

"You're obsessive," he states. Not as a question, but almost as an approval. As if I passed a test I didn't know I was taking.

"You don't pursue one thing you're entire life because of a passing interest," I add.

He grazes his finger over my flute, to my violin, and then the steel drum as if he is checking for dust. He won't find any. I have all of them laid out and mounted on the wall like this so I am reminded of them anytime I create a new song. It's the same thing my mom does with her spices, so she doesn't forget to use them. And for me, it's effective. None of my instruments go untouched for long.

His fingers hover over my most used ingredient, the salt of my songs- my acoustic guitar.

"May I?" he says.

My heart flutters a bit at this. Mostly because he asked. I can't count the amount of times some self-entitled Tinder date has taken her off the wall and starting strumming her without asking.

"You may. In fact, I demand it. You have something to prove to me, remember?" I take a step closer. "And if you're lying, now is the time to fess up because I'll be seriously pissed off if I let you play her and you don't know what you're doing... She deserves more than that."

He smirks and I remember the cocky devil I'm dealing with.

"I won't play her exactly the way you play her, but I'll pay attention to every brush of my fingers so I learn what it takes to make her really sing," he says with a glint in his eyes. I'm not so sure we're talking about my guitar anymore.

"Stop delaying," I say, avoiding his gaze out of fear of what my face might reveal right now.

I sit in the wooden chair across from my grey couch that he's lowered himself into.

He clears his throat and settles my guitar into himself. He looks comfortable with it, and I'm starting to believe he might actually know what he's doing. His striking face turns back up to me and I experience that dopamine rush from seeing him head on all over again.

"I dedicate this to you, dear Mel. Even though you won't tell me why you've had a bad day."

He strums a familiar tune, and I swallow hard because I recognize it immediately. One of my favorites.

He whispers the beginning of the song, which is a series of "la-la-las" and for a second I wonder if he's shy about his singing voice.

Then he sings the first lines of "Wild World" by Cat Stevens simply and confidently.

There's not a single thing in this world that's more of an aphrodisiac to me than a song well sung. Now here I am, in my apartment alone with a man who looks like that and happens to be singing one of my favorite songs to me. It's like I've created my own perfect honey trap to catch myself in.

He gets to the chorus and I cross my legs in an attempt to look composed even though I can actually feel myself swooning.

Suddenly he does something sexier than I could have ever anticipated. Something that shows this man plays dirty and with no mercy. He switches the damn lyrics to French.

I practically melt into a pool onto the floor, hearing how seamlessly he switches to the language. The specks of his accent that now infuse the song turn the sentimental lyrics into something that sounds utterly dirty to me.

I let my eyes meet his and the way he is looking at me scares the hell out of me. His stare is unwavering and greedy, and I don't think I have the power to not give him what he wants, if what he wants turns out to be me.

I swallow deeply and I see his tongue dart out of his mouth to wet his red lower lip as he strums the chords. That's the last straw.

I stand up. He immediately places the guitar next to him as if on command, and joins me standing.

"You proved your point," I say in a low breathless whisper.

"You know that's not why I really came here," he answers gruffly.

He steps towards me, and my chest constricts in nervousness about what I think is about to happen between us, two complete strangers. He moves his long fingers along the edge of my cheek. His gentle touch traces down my neck and twists around the strap of my camisole as my sweater slides off of my shoulder. My heart races at his forwardness, debating what I want.

But the answer is obvious. I want to get lost in this man. I pull both my sweater and camisole over my head in a quick motion so I am standing in my powder-blue lace bra before him. His eyes trace the contours of my body and I like the fire I see in them.

I unbutton the top of his shirt and he helps by starting at the bottom. When it's done, I trace my fingers down his muscled arms to slide his shirt off him. I follow the lines of his muscled chest and abdomen down to the small tuft of hair leading down under his expensive looking belt. The sight sends pure, instinctual lust through me.

We both paw at each other to remove our bottoms, him struggling with the old, stiff zipper on my skirt.

Finally, we are standing in only our underwear, baring ourselves to each other. Somehow this feels right, like we need to make ourselves vulnerable to each other before we start whatever it is we're about to start, because we've been throwing barbs at each other all night. By stripping down, we concede that we're both willing to be at the mercy of the other.

I trace my eyes up his body. He is built lean and tall but has enough muscle to have a thickness to his tall frame. I like him even more without all the pretentiousness of his nice clothing.

He seems to like me too, as he reaches down into his boxer briefs to reign in the large bulge that is growing between us. I don't comment on the thick outline that I'm pretty sure I'm staring at, but I want to. I want to shake his hand and congratulate him for being so deliciously proportioned all over.

"You're beautiful, Melody." Of all the times this evening, he chooses now to use my full name. I swallow hard at the earnestness in his face. He moves his fingers under my chin and coaxes my face to his.

I close my eyes, expecting a kiss, but when it doesn't come, I look to see what is taking so long. Lucien's face is lowered as if he moved in to kiss me, but froze. I see now that his face is twisted in pain.

Instead of explaining what the hell is going on, he runs to the kitchen garbage. And there my naked, erect, beautiful guest throws up all the picklebacks he so enthusiastically shot back in the hours before.

I take a deep sigh of resignation. This fits exactly with the day I've been having. I'm not sure why I let myself expect anything more.

CHAPTER FOUR
Melody

"Lucifer!" I try yelling at the hulking man fast asleep in my bed. When that doesn't even cause him to stir, I resort to pushing at him. My sheets barely cover his long, muscled body and I have to resist the temptation to stop and admire how effortlessly sexy he is even when in a hungover coma. He groans but doesn't even try to open his eyes.

Desperate times call for desperate measures. I run to the kitchen and let the faucet run on the coldest setting while I fill up a glass with ice. I add water and rush back to the bedroom.

Bombs away. I throw the water over him.

"Merde! Fuck! Shit!"

Mission accomplished.

Lucien's hulking body sits up in attention, ready to fend off the evil creature attacking him, a.k.a. me.

"What the hell are you doing?" He growls while holding his head. Apparently his jerking reaction was too rough for his liquor-soaked body.

"You wouldn't wake up! My family lives nearby and they are insisting on coming over. They're going to be here in ten minutes tops," I say frantically while searching for his clothes on the floor.

I'm not sure why I thought drowning my sorrows in whiskey, pickle juice, and this man was a good idea. Usually whiskey and pickle juice work just fine. Did I really have to throw him in as an extra ingredient?

And do I really hate that I did? This morning is a more sober reassurance that this man is sexy as hell. His long muscled body, dark hair, and dark stubble make it as if the Wikipedia entry for "tall, dark, and handsome" is curled up in my bed.

But it isn't his looks that make him still, admittedly, interesting to me. It's the hunger I sense burning in him. A hunger that allowed him to be my partner in abandoning the world for at least one night and along with it, the normal and polite ways of society.

And, oh man, were we about to abandon all politeness before he tossed his cookies for about an hour straight. There was that one moment, before it all went downhill, that even the alcohol couldn't fog up. The moment that made it clear how badly he wanted to get lost in me, like I wanted to get lost in him.

Yet, the cost of picklebacks demanded to be repaid.

Luckily for me, after his puking, he wasn't the slightest bit shy about staying in his boxer-briefs only. But I don't blame him. If I were him, I would walk around naked all the time. It seems only fair to let people know he is no ordinary man; he is an ideal specimen. The kind of man you wouldn't have believed existed without proof- long, lean, and thick where it counts.

But in the harsh light of the morning, any dream of getting lost in this man is over. *Very* over, as the loud ringtone this morning of my mom calling made clear.

Lucien rubs his eyes and smirks when he sees me. I have a towel on from my shower and I am standing a foot away from the edge of the bed with the glass full of ice water still lifted in position to attack at any moment.

With a quick movement, he grabs the glass out of my hand and places it on my nightstand table. He grabs me by the waist, flings me back onto the bed and lays his body over mine, slipping his fingers into mine.

I can smell the whiskey on his breath, but it's mixed with his cologne and somehow the scent fills me with pleasure rather than disgust. That probably also has to do with the fact that he brushed his teeth with a spare toothbrush about five times after his little episode.

"Well, I can't wait to meet the family," he says with a mischievous smile.

"Hell no." I slip out from under him, despite the heat I feel rushing through me from being under his body.

I stand up quickly and go back to the glass of water, which has proven to be a very effective tool.

"I'll do it!" I warn.

"I'm not a dog," he says, glaring at me. But to my relief, he gets up and begins putting his clothes on.

Not quickly enough, though. My doorbell rings and I curse. I frantically pull some clothes on and ignore Lucien's smile as I am half-naked again.

"Don't look!" I scold him.

He rolls his eyes and finishes pulling up his pants as I throw a sweater over my bra.

I push him out of my bedroom, and the doorbell rings again.

"Okay, just pretend you're a neighbor or something as you walk down the stairs," I direct him as he finishes pulling on his cognac leather shoes. I practically shove him out the front door as my hand lingers on the buzzer to let my family in.

"Is this any way to treat a one-night-stand?" Lucien says with an eyebrow cocked.

"You don't get to call me that," I cross my arms. "You have to not spew in someone's apartment to call someone that. Oh, and actually have sex." I add, in case he doesn't know what happened last night, which is possible given the amount we drank.

I think I detect a slight look of surprise at this, but rather than addressing it, he leans in and kisses me on the cheek and lingers, his face close to mine. "Thanks for last night. And whatever drove you to be my partner in self-sabotage, I have every confidence that you'll be fine. With that voice and that attitude, you've got the world at your fingers, Mel."

I pause at this, observing his face. His demeanor surprises me. We've been jabbing at each other since we met, but his tone now is gentle and sincere. Then my heart drops at the reality of what he's saying. The whole reason I had gone down this rabbit hole with him was to block out the fact that I don't have a future in front of me anymore. At least, not the future I thought I had.

With him leaving, I officially can't hide from it anymore. My family is about to be here to console me over the fact that my dream of getting a record contract was in the palm of my hand, before being ripped out by some overeager heir trying to prove himself as the new head of his family business. It only took one nepotistic douchebag to stomp all over my dreams.

"Yeah, thanks." I shrug. "And I have every confidence you'll meet either a nice lady with an actual soul soon or the gold-digger of your dreams when your 87, depending on what you want." I give him a weak smile at this, because I'm really not sure which one he would prefer. He doesn't look so sure either.

"Alright, remember to pretend you're my neighbor when you pass my family on your way out," I say pushing him out the door again.

He nods and pulls himself back. He pauses for a second to look up at me. My face silently asks him what the hell he is waiting for, but before I can, he turns to go down the stairs.

I take a big breath of relief and ignore the nagging feeling of disappointment that he's actually leaving.

I buzz my family in and I hear them opening the big metal door leading into my apartment building.

"Hello," Lucien's voice echoes up the stairway. *Oh, god.* "I'm Mel's neighbor and I'm headed out for a walk," he says as if reading from a script, no doubt intentionally meaning to sound as suspicious as possible.

"Uh, okay." I can hear my mom answer with confusion. "Well, enjoy."

Really nice, Lucifer. Of course, he couldn't resist one last jab at me.

CHAPTER FIVE
Lucien

I settle into my leather chair at my desk, freshly showered in my office shower without bothering to go home this morning. Even though I could have come in late as I'm the boss, there are inevitable fires that need putting out at work because of the harsh measures I had to take yesterday. Last night was not meant to be an all-nighter in some beautiful pink-haired stranger's apartment, and it especially wasn't meant to be spent puking rather than fucking.

Yet, I feel good. Considering yesterday started as a shitty day at work, progressed to me getting dumped humiliatingly, and ended with me spewing my guts ingloriously, I would even say I'm fucking fantastic. I can't remember the last time I sang in front of someone. I can't remember the last time someone made me so god damn horny. And I certainly can't remember the last time someone was so *combative* with me. Somehow that last part makes me even more horny.

Before I get started, I need to make sure I see this girl again. Even if she ends up like every other woman who just wants something from me, at least for a brief moment, she might make me feel like this again. Or relieve this aching erection that hasn't been able to calm down since the bar.

I grabbed a picture of the list of last names on the mailboxes on my way out. She has to be one of these, and the internet would quickly tell me which one.

I call for Barb, my secretary, to come in.

"Good Morning, Barb. Thanks for coming in early today."

"Part of the job, sir." Barb says matter-of-factly, and she means it. Her no nonsense demeanor is a part of why my decision to hire her was so ingenious on my part. Barb Mavis is a mother of four kids who all grew up and flew the coop, and she decided to start working again. My H.R. Department was eager to dismiss her as a non-starter, but after dozens of assistants who would take any opportunity to "prove themselves" as some music industry savant instead of doing the actual job they were hired for, I grabbed onto Barb's application like a lifeline.

And it worked. She makes no charade about what she wants, she just likes the work day-to-day and buying herself expensive things with her hard earned money. When I'm being an asshole, she calls it like it is because she's got nothing of grave importance to lose. If anything, Barb has become the hot commodity between us and I would do anything not to lose her.

"I have a small sleuth job for you." I pull out my phone and show her the mailboxes. "Would you mind searching all these last names with the first name 'Melody' until you find a pink-haired musical ingenue? I'll send the picture over to you now."

"No problem, Mr. De la Roche. Is that all for now?" She insists on still addressing me like this, even though I've asked her repeatedly to call me Luc. I think she probably knows I secretly like it.

"That's it for now." She nods in confirmation and heads out the door. "Wonderful new necklace though, Barb. Don't think I didn't notice."

She turns around with a smile, clutching the shimmering diamonds at her neck. "I figured I should buy myself what I really want *before* the holidays this year, so on Christmas morning I don't get disappointed when my husband and kids present me with the vacuum they all pitched in to get."

I grin at this. "That's the logic I hired you for. Which reminds me, schedule a time on Monday for us to discuss your Christmas bonus. Maybe you'll want the matching earrings for that necklace?"

This makes her grin even wider. "Oh, trust me, Mr. De la Roche, I *do*. Monday it is," she says with a wink before she closes my office door.

The morning passes quickly, mostly because I decided to not read any press about me. The bad press will be a double hit with the gossip magazines covering my break-up while the trade magazines will have written about the ruthless contract binge I finalized yesterday. I'll let the P.R. Department come up with a plan of attack before I worry myself about all of it. Instead, I am devoting today to making sure none of the artists with cancelled contracts are trying to sue me while bolstering the confidence among the remaining artists so they know they have stability with De la Roche Records.

So far, no lawsuits, but many insecure artists who did not get their contracts cut. As I finish an e-mail to the marketing department to request they amp up efforts for our current artists, Barb knocks on the door.

It's perfect timing because my next order of business is to order the gift I've decided I'll send to Melody. Despite an impressive collection of instruments, I noticed she doesn't have a lute, a string-instrument prized in France's history. Sure, it might be a little forward to send a two thousand dollar instrument after knowing someone for only one night, but really it's just an apology for puking in her apartment.

"Here is Miss Greco's file," Barb announces, holding up a manilla folder with a company tab on it.

I look at her with confusion. "Thanks, but you didn't need to make a file for her, Barb. A simple name would have been sufficient."

She returns my look of confusion with her own.

"Sir, I didn't make the file. It already existed. Melody Greco had a contract with De la Roche Records."

I swallow hard. This must be some kind of misunderstanding.

"*Had* a contract?" I ask hesitantly.

"Yes, Mr. De la Roche. Before yesterday's purge." She used the word I had used, 'purge', to describe the mass cancelling of contracts, but after last night it sounds like an ironic jeer at me.

"There must be some sort of confusion. Melody Greco? She has pink hair? Somewhere in her twenties?" I ask through a suddenly dry mouth.

Barb opens the file and examines it, nods, and places it on my desk. "I believe this is the woman you're looking for, but if it's not, I'll start my search again."

I open the folder and clipped to the back of the cover is a photo. There is no doubt it is the same Melody that cracked me open last night and made me come alive for the first time in a long time.

Yet, I might have had trouble recognizing the girl in this photo if I hadn't so obsessively studied the slopes and lines of her face. The girl in this photo has the most genuine beaming smile, almost infantile in its hope and joy. The Melody I met yesterday had a much more protected gaze, as if someone had taken that youthful naïveté and smashed it into a million pieces in front of her.

And I have a sinking realization that 'someone', is *me*.

CHAPTER SIX
Melody

"Since when do you have a handsome, businessman neighbor?" my little sister Julia looks at me from across the restaurant table with a sparkle in her eye. She's still in high school but is eager to grow up, and there is no mistaking the fact that she is trying to expose my bad decision-making to our parents right now.

"What are you talking about?" I feign ignorance, which is always the best option for my family.

"There was a man that passed us on the way out that smelled like a distillery and strangely, an overwhelming amount of dill, almost like pickles," my dad adds. I stifle a laugh. Hopefully, my shower got off my own matching "strange" smell.

I lift one shoulder to pretend I'm bored by the conversation, "I don't know everyone in my building yet."

"Okay, *Mel*," my sister emphasizes my nickname. Crap, I forgot he used my name on the way out. My parents luckily don't seem to notice.

"Well, that is for the better since you might not be staying there for long," my mom says, wasting no time making me feel horrible. Not on purpose, of course. She's hoped that I would move back home before the devastating news of my contract being cancelled. Yet, the reality of her words reveals the deeper truth of my situation, and suddenly it might be my turn to barf up whiskey and pickle juice.

"I'll get another job. I'll book double gigs. I'll do whatever I have to do," I say, fighting back tears. My contract cancellation isn't only a devastation because of what I'm missing out on, but also because I thought my family finally didn't need to worry about me anymore. I thought I had proven to them I would not be the starving artist they fear I will become. But clearly, their fear is very much still present. Hustling for gigs and making music in my free time has no guarantee of a steady income.

"My girl," my dad starts with tenderness in his voice. He's always been a bit more gentle than my mom, but no less strict. They play good cop, bad cop, well. "You're not a failure if you need to move back in. In fact, you're so fortunate that your parents live in this city."

There it is. If my dad wants me to move home as well, then that should be all the verification I need that they are truly worried for me. He's right that I'm lucky they live in Brooklyn. But my apartment is also where I make my music. When I moved into my own space, it allowed me to come into my own and express myself without being interrupted. I swallow down the anxious truth that pops to the surface but can't face right now- that I am making *music* per se, but not the strong lyrics that I need to make me stand out. I've only been any good at creating instrumentals and hoping the lyrics come later. But they will never come if I live under my parents' roof again.

"You don't want me home," I try a different tactic. "I've grown even more messy and much louder than the little girl you used to know. Do you want to wake up to me strumming the guitar at 6 A.M.?"

"Yeah, and the room is my glam room now," Julia adds. Glam room? I don't have time to question what the hell a glam room is, and just nod my head in agreement as if this is an extremely important point.

"Can you even pay next month's rent?" My mom asks. "We can't help you again."

It's the 'again' that skewers me. I hate that they ever had to help me. Both of their parents, my grandparents, were immigrants and they had to fight for every single penny they have.

"I'll be able to," I say with enough hesitance that I am almost admitting defeat. Luckily, the server unknowingly provides the perfect distraction from me as he drops our meals off at the table. The smell of my favorite lasagna brings me some much needed vitality.

I use the moment to check my e-mail on my phone under the table as a last waning hope. Maybe I've heard from one of the booking agents I frantically reached out to yesterday about doing shows over the holidays. I could at least feed my parents some assurance with one of those morsels.

No e-mails from the usual agents are in my box, but there is an e-mail from someone I don't recognize with a strange title, 'Lapland Booking'. I click on it with a desperate urgency.

It's a request to book me for a week at a hotel in northern Finland. The payment is considerably more than my standard rate. The only catch is that I would leave the day after Christmas, but that's not too bad at all. Especially because that's when the first payment would come in for the gig, taking care of my rent money. Of course, the other problem is that this seems too good to be true, and could be a scam. *Whatever*, I can figure that out later.

"I'll be able to when I get the payment for my big job at the end of the month," I continue in my smoothest possible attempt, hoping they don't realize this save just came from my inbox and for all I know is a spam e-mail to fleece my credit card information or even my kidney.

"What big job?" My mom says through skeptical, narrowed eyes.

"The day after Christmas I'm flying to Finland," I deadpan as if this is the most natural sentence ever, "for a big gig at a hotel opening."

"All the way to *where*? And already on the day after Christmas? You're going to be away from us on Christmas?" My mother's eyes are big and dramatic now.

"Mom, how many times do I have to say that the day after Christmas isn't Christmas," I sigh. This is a surprisingly prevalent conversation between us. Every time I so much as change out of my Christmas pajamas on the 26th, she takes it as a direct attack.

"Plus, it pays well. So I'll be set for at the next couple months," my heart races at this news as I say it. If this booking is legit, then it is the miracle I need. It will give me enough of a cushion to spend time looking for a new record deal or at least finally finish the lyrics for a song. Hey, maybe the Finnish cold will even inspire me?

"How long will you be gone? Can I use your apartment?" Julia pipes up.

"If you get me a really nice Christmas present, I'll think about it."

And at last, this is enough to steer the conversation away from me so I can finally dig into my lasagna in peace.

CHAPTER SEVEN
Lucien

I get off the phone with my driver, Mark, who confirmed that he delivered my present to Melody. It's the morning of Christmas Eve, so I thanked him for his last duty of the year and wished him happy holidays.

I'm sitting in my penthouse and supposed to be reading over contracts. Instead, I've been staring into the fireplace waiting for news about the delivery for a concerning amount of time. Along with the lute, I included a note explaining who I am- the man who recently cancelled her contract and likely crushed her dreams. It took me a couple days of deliberation, but ultimately I wanted to get ahead of her finding out some other way.

After some more pathetic staring, I decide I can reach out to Melody, rather than hope she reaches out to me on the number I provided her. It isn't a completely emotional decision. After all, if she forgives me she might not sue De la Roche Records for breach of contract. She would inevitably lose the lawsuit and with it, thousands of dollars, so I'm actually doing her a favor. And sure, I've thought about her eyes alight with passion and her body in nothing but her lace underwear far more times than I care to admit.

But that's just a bonus.

There is a risk that when she finds out who I am, that sassy woman will disappear and she will become the malleable, people-pleaser that most people become when they glimpse a hint of power in the person they're talking to. The thought makes me sick.

I wait a little longer to see if she will contact me. Maybe she'll call me gushing over how much she loves the lute as an addition to her instrument wall.

Just sit and wait, looking over these contracts. No big deal. I'm sure any second now, I'll hear from her.

Oh, fuck it. If you want a job done, do it yourself. I pull up the number I got from her file on my phone.

Me: Merry Christmas Eve, Mel.

Melody: Is this Lucifer De la Roche? Because if it is, I'm blocking you.

I can't help but smirk at this. I can't believe for a second that I thought her attitude might go away when she knows who I am.

Me: As the note said, I'm really sorry about your contract. I didn't know who you were when I met you.

Three dots show that she's typing and then stop. Crap. They start again and her text finally comes through.

Melody: Let me be absolutely clear- I would never have invited you into my home if I knew who you were. You're a callous and entitled heir who is clearly adiaphorous at best toward the soul of music. I want nothing to do with you.

I shouldn't be grinning even wider. She is probably furious, and what she is saying has a lot of truth to it.

Me: Ah, so you got that clue in the New York Times crossword too? It was a tricky one. Tell the truth, did you know 'adiaphorous' before solving all the surrounding words?

Melody: Go back to hell, Lucifer. Or maybe you don't need to bother because no doubt the world you inhabit is just as soulless.

I look around at my empty apartment, the place where I'll be spending Christmas Eve and Christmas and actually feel the cut of her words. My father is off in the Cayman Islands with some random woman for the holidays. My mother and younger sister, Marie, are in France, which I couldn't join because I need to finish work in New York before I leave on an investment-related vacation on the 26th. I invited them to join me on my upcoming trip, but they declined. Marie and I spent our childhood going back and forth from France and New York between our mother's and father's. Since we've become adults, it's as if we've split into two families. They probably don't want to spend time with me because all they see when they look at me is my father, and in that case, I don't blame them for not wanting to spend a vacation with me. I wouldn't want to spend a vacation with a facsimile of my father either.

Melody: If you tell me why you cut my contract, I'll delay blocking you.

Me: Unfortunately, it's more complicated than a simple text. I could explain it all to you if you let me take you to dinner.

Melody: I would rather go on a date with the puke you left in my kitchen.

Me: Awe, that's sweet. You want to get to know all my parts, the good and the bad.

Melody: I'm blocking you.

Me: Wait, just hear me out.

Melody: The number you are trying to contact does not exist.

I pause, staring down at the text.

Me: You just typed that in, didn't you?

No response. I wait, staring down at the screen. When three dots show up and I actually laugh out loud at her ridiculousness.

Melody: Only until I figure out how to actually block you, which I will 100% be doing.

Me: Okay, fine. But in the meantime, I'm going to send you links to all of my favorite performances so you can fall desperately in love with our compatibility and my taste in music.

She doesn't respond, so I go to YouTube and begin copying and pasting the links to my favorite videos of live performances. I have an arsenal already ready because I've been thinking about what she might enjoy from the moment I saw her on stage. And fine, I checked out her YouTube page, which is mostly covers of other songs, but it made me realize that she enjoys a lot of the same music I do. I barrage her with songs that I consider the peak of music, as well as lesser known performances of the songs that we both seem to like.

Finally, the cherry on top, if I say so myself, is sending a link of her own performance of "Wild World" from her YouTube page. I want her to know that I saw the description she wrote on the video remarking how this is one of her favorite songs of all time. It's also the song I sang to her in her apartment. I had unknowingly serenaded her with one of her favorite songs. No wonder she practically tore her clothes off. What I don't tell her is that it's also one of my favorite songs. She doesn't need to know that.

I also keep it to myself that I think her version of it does it justice. Hell, it does it more than justice, it's perfect. Only seeing the thumbnail pop up on my screen of her face under the title of the song makes me need to listen to it for the hundredth time since I found it.

But that's simply because I love music, I remind myself. Why am I acting like she's my damn soul mate or something?

To balance things out, I send a performance by Eminem to show her I'm not some soft gooey man who has watched her YouTube channel obsessively.

And this time my message has a vicious red exclamation point next to it.

Not Delivered.

And there is no mistaking, this time she really blocked me.

CHAPTER EIGHT
Melody

Christmas passed too quickly, as Christmas always does. For a long time, what made Christmas so joyful was having a tiny Julia running around like a maniac because Santa came. She's outgrown that for about half a decade now, but I still haven't gotten over the tug of nostalgia that we don't have a little one in the family anymore.

Last year was the only year I had a boyfriend during Christmas. Music is a jealous and demanding boyfriend all on its own, not leaving much room for someone in my life who isn't equally as obsessive as me. So far that person doesn't exist, but last year I gave it a shot with Clark, a guy I met at Bowie's who was an aspiring actor. The relationship ended after about 6 months, but since it fell over Christmas, my mom had no problem laying out a future where little Clarks and Melodys would run around, looking for clues from Santa. But this year was noticeably absent of any kind of suggestion that one day I might be responsible for children. Considering I barely had enough money to get my family gifts, I can understand why.

But today starts the first day on the path to making rent. My

Finland gig is officially underway. The gig that I will give 200% into because it saved me from an early and forced retirement from music. Of course, I wouldn't give up on my music career because of one asshole. In fact, I wouldn't give up on my music career even if I was 90-years-old and tone deaf. But the reality is, I need money.

Once I learned this gig isn't a scam, I became even more excited about the opportunity to come to a country I've never been and stay in a fancy hotel. Apparently the booker had seen one of my Brooklyn shows and then checked out my YouTube channel and thought I had the perfect vibe for the opening of this hotel.

Now, after a trip so long that I'm pretty sure I can classify it as torture, I finally arrive at the hotel and wonder what exactly they saw in my vibe that they found to be perfect. The place is luxurious, decadent, and expensive. Three things *I* am not.

Even in the pitch black, it's clear that the hotel is beautiful from the outside. It has modern lines that are balanced by wood and slate building materials.

I pass through the glass door to the opening of the lobby, which has marble floors, copper fixtures, and smells like lemongrass. I read online that this is only one part of the hotel. There is this large main building and then there are glass "igloo" cabins that are spread throughout the grounds for aurora watching. I probably won't see any of those cabins throughout my stay, as they are the luxury rooms and the price tag listed on their website for one night could feed me for a year.

I step further into the lobby and look around, a little lost, until I am greeted by a smiling blonde girl at the front desk.

"Tervetuloa!" she says enthusiastically.

"Uh," I blink at her, still bleary from the flight. "That means 'welcome' right?" I tried to brush up on basic Finnish phrases on the plane ride and gave up after reading 'nice to meet you' is approximately 1,000 letters long and I'm pretty sure all vowels.

"Impressive," she responds with a smile. "That's more Finnish than most people know. How can I help you?"

"I'm here as a performer. My name is Melody Greco."

"Of course! I thought so. Welcome to Puro Hotel, Melody. We're so excited to have you. We even watched some of your YouTube videos. I absolutely *loved* your cover of 'Blank Space'."

I love this girl already. Being recognized by a stranger for my music has happened, well, never.

"You really know how to butter a girl up. I'll be sure to play that then if you come to see me preform. What's your name?"

"Oh, I apologize." She says as she comes out from behind the counter. "My name is Lumi. It means snow. As if there isn't enough here already." She says with a laugh. What an awesome name.

She extends her hand, and I take it. She seems younger than me, but not by too much. I am suddenly very grateful to have such a friendly acquaintance in this place on the edge of the world.

She moves back behind the desk to scan my passport and then hands me over a hotel card key and explains that I have money on it to get meals, snacks, and drinks from the hotel bar and restaurant during my stay. That's certainly a nice perk.

But also a little lonely, as I imagine I'll be eating by myself. I'm okay with spending time alone, but just yesterday I was celebrating Christmas with my family and it feels like the warmth of the holiday was ripped off like a band-aid. I shake the thought away. This is good money and I'm doing what I love. It's worth it, and there is no sense in wallowing.

I get ready to navigate towards my room.

"Hey," Lumi starts before I walk off. "My shift is done in 20 minutes and I was going to get my staff meal at the restaurant if you want to join?"

"That would be great," I sigh in relief. "I can meet you there then?"

Lumi nods, smiling at my obvious excitement from her invitation.

Yes, I confirm again with myself. This is going to be a great week. It will be full of music, recovering my bank account, and an added bonus of finally being far enough away from Lucifer De la Roche so he has to stay the hell out of my life.

CHAPTER NINE
Melody

My hotel room is simple but luxurious, draped in cream fabrics with pops of sage and hunter green. The window looks out to pine trees coated in snow that peak open to reveal an icy river, lit by lampposts that line a riverside path so it can be enjoyed even in the dark. And there is certainly no shortage of darkness here in the winter. The Welcome Packet clarified that there's actually a little less than 3 hours of actual daylight at this time of the year which according to them means all the more opportunity to see the northern lights. Apparently, they're optimists, just like I'm trying to be and on this particular point- I'm sold. If I see the northern lights, this might quickly become one of the best weeks ever.

I unpack and hang up some small holiday decorations my mom insisted I take with me even though Christmas is over. I immediately am glad I do. The hotel room is so much more personal with our homemade stars hanging in the windows.

I freshen up quickly with a quick rinse and a change of clothes and by the time I finish, it's already time to meet Lumi. I hurry into the elevator and follow the signs until I find the dining area.

The restaurant has a blazing fire and sturdy wooden candlelit tables spread across the slate floor. The vast space seems to operate as half restaurant and bar, and half common room. Where one half has people dining, the other half looks like a lounge and is full of cozy places for people to sit. There is a family tucked away on a leather couch playing a board game and my heart tugs wondering what my family is doing. Before I can reflect too long over that, I spot Lumi at a table next to a floor-to-ceiling window that looks out to the river.

Sitting and chatting with Lumi feels natural and easy. I immediately get swept up in asking her all about Finland. She insisted I get the salmon soup when we ordered, and now that it's in front of me, I decide to trust her completely with all my decisions while I'm here. The soup is absolutely delicious. It's somehow rich, creamy, and fresh all at the same time. It reminds me of the clam chowder I grew up getting on Long Island but with bright fresh pink pieces of salmon and fresh dill instead.

"So, what do you do in your free time, Lumi?" I finally ask after I realize I've been so concentrated on ladling this soup into my mouth that I let the conversation drop.

She laughs. "You know, for Finns it's not weird to sit with each other in silence. Don't worry if you would just rather eat your soup. I'm sure you're starving."

I *am* starving. But I also want to learn about my one and only friend within a 10-hour flight radius.

"That's okay. Pleasant conversation makes the food taste better. If that's even possible." I say with a smile, before immediately spooning a gigantic piece of buttery potato in my mouth.

"Well, it's a little embarrassing, actually."

I nod in encouragement. 'A little embarrassing' is always a promising start.

"I also love music. I promise, I didn't just invite you to stalk you or something like that."

I laugh at this. As if I am worried about having super-fans.

"I promise I don't think you're a stalker. I'm pretty sure you have to be famous to be stalked by strangers."

"But you are famous! You have thousands of followers! Maybe that's not a big deal to you, but I'd give up my little brother to get that many views."

I both laugh and cringe at this. I laugh at the vision of Lumi handing over a little blonde boy to some music executives, but cringe at the fact that my lack of progress despite my followers has made it all the way across the ocean. She believes what I had also believed, that persistence can make a career. Yet here I am, on the cusp of having to give up my dream forever. I can't even hide from my career stalemate in the Arctic?

"Well, I guess I'm just a little lost lately. I'm having trouble getting a solid music career going," I admit. She should know the reality of this life if she's interested in it. "But anyway, regarding your music, I would love to hear your stuff if you want to send it to me. Or we can have a jam session or something. I'll just be here waiting until my shows in the evening, so I'll have time."

She nods with a smile. "I'd love that."

I see her eyes dart up quickly to watch something behind me with interest.

I look at her questioningly.

"You have some compatriots here," she explains. "Some fellow Americans. We've been calling them the Black Card Crew because they all seem to be ridiculously wealthy. One of the girls is the owner of the hotel. And don't look now, but the tall, dark-haired guy is Lucien De la Roche. The guy is filthy rich, like billionaire rich, and looks like *that*. This world isn't fair sometimes."

I drop the soup spoon, splashing white broth everywhere. I couldn't have heard that right. No, I must be having some kind of episode.

"I'm sorry, I must have heard you incorrectly. Did you say Lucien De la Roche?" I decide to just get the question out of the way so my heart rate can calm down. My new friend might think I'm out of my mind, hearing things and scared of a big invisible devil who isn't even here.

"Yeah! You know of him? There was a big thing in our staff meeting about how we should not slip him any demo material. Apparently, it happens to him a lot."

I accidentally inhale the water I took a sip of to calm down and begin coughing like a maniac. My heart races and for a second I feel like I might stop breathing. Is it really possible that this damn man has managed to track me all the way here? What else would be the explanation? Was it De la Roche Records who was behind my booking just to add insult to injury?

I turn slowly to subtly check out the group that supposedly includes Satan himself but can't get a good enough glimpse without being obvious.

I turn back to face Lumi as they walk our way. They're heading past us toward the fire.

I trail my eyes on them and I spot the back of a tall, dark-haired figure that twists my stomach into a knot and sends a burst of adrenaline run through me.

How is this possible?

Did the universe decide I was being too optimistic and is balancing it out to make me feel like absolute shit again?

"You okay?" Lumi asks.

I realize I am fully staring.

"I… I know him."

And at that moment, the man's eyes dart up at me as if he recognized my voice. As soon as I see him, I recognize it is the same man who made me feel beautiful and hungry under his gaze for one night. But now, seeing him for the first time knowing who he actually is, all I can think about is how this is the man who crushed my dreams, Lucien De la Roche, the head of De la Roche Records.

The recognition unfolds on his face when we lock eyes and to my surprise he looks just as confused as I am.

He wastes no time pacing right toward me.

"Oh yeah, I dare you, Lucifer," I whisper under my breath.

I watch him approach with a steely gaze. I resent the way every female eye in the place latches on to him. He doesn't deserve it. They wouldn't look at him that way if they knew what kind of man he is. The kind who goes back on their word. The kind who doesn't give two craps about what's right, only profit. *I* wouldn't have looked at him that way if I had known.

"Melody," his gruff and slightly accented voice booms from behind Lumi and she jumps in surprise, looking wide-eyed between the two of us. "Are you stalking me?" His low voice accuses me.

I stare at him in horror at his audacity and then make a sound somewhere between a scoff and a laugh. I stand up to not seem so small beneath him, but when I do, he still towers over me. I cross my arms indignantly. "Like I would ever willingly be in the same place as you! You're the one who's followed me to the middle of the Arctic at the very hotel I'm preforming at this week. Why? Is this some sick game?"

"Wait, you're preforming here?" He says, motioning to the room we're in.

I nod yes as if it's the most obvious thing in the world and return to my glare of utter disdain.

He takes a sigh in resignation. "Come with me," he commands.

"Hell no! I'm trying to enjoy dinner and not get fired for reaming you out."

"It looks like you've enjoyed dinner already," he motions to my bowl. "Just come with me for one second over there. I think I know what happened."

I look at my soup. There are still at least three hot spoonfuls left and I am not about to abandon this delicious creation for this poor excuse of a human.

"I'm having dinner with my friend right now and I'm going to finish it," I say with finality.

He takes a deep and frustrated sigh. "Just as infuriating as the day I met you, I see."

I shrug. "Must be why you came all the way to the North Pole to find me."

"This isn't the North Pole, *Mel*." He says, clearly proud of himself for using the name I told him not to, instead of being embarrassed for not understanding hyperbole. "I'll be back," he says gruffly and marches away from me.

I don't even acknowledge his exit while I sit down to take another sip of my soup. As I'm savoring the last moment of my delicious new favorite food, I finally glance up only to see Lumi's mouth slack and her eyes practically popping out of her head.

"You just blew off *Lucien De la Roche*?" she whispers, as if saying Santa Claus isn't real in a room full of kids.

"He's a jerk. Handsome billionaire, or not."

Now Lucien is storming back my way with his friend that I recognize from the night we met. I don't recall his name and we didn't get a chance to talk very much. He was too busy making out with Ryan, which made me like him at the time, but now he's nothing but a traitor fraternizing with the other side.

"Melody, darling," the friend walks out in front of Lucien and extends his hand. This time I stand up to be polite and Lumi joins me. I pretend not to notice Lucien's eyes tracing up my body. "I don't think we formally met, just kind of drunkenly huffed at each other. My name is Cole." We shake hands and I introduce Lumi.

Lucien growls, "and…"

"And I booked you. You're very talented and our friend Brooke was looking for entertainment for the official opening here."

"Oh!" I say, genuinely surprised. I hadn't dealt with anyone named Cole, so I suspect it was his secretary I was communicating with. "Well, thank you so much for including me in this. It's really wonderful to be here."

"Oh, it turns out you do have the capacity to be sweet when you want to be," Lucien says with a grin.

I don't acknowledge him, as that seems the wisest course of action.

"Someone say my name?" A young brunette woman glides over to us. She's beautiful in an elegant and understated way. Her wealth is apparent immediately but not because she's glitzy but because everything on her is clearly high quality, from the dewy makeup on her face to the cashmere sweater she's wearing.

"Oh, hey Lumi!" She says when she gets close enough to see Lumi standing next to me. I give her credit for knowing someone's name who works here. In my experience, that's certainly more than most wealthy people do.

She extends her hand to me, "I'm Brooke. You must be the amazing Melody that Cole told me about."

"Oh, well, I hope to live up to his praise. So, you're the owner of Puro Hotel?"

She nods. "Well, yes, of Melo Hotel Group. But these fine gentlemen here are both investors in this project, so you could consider them the owners as well."

"You can call me Boss Lucifer, Mel," Lucien says with a self-satisfied grin.

Brooke rolls her eyes and I instantly like her even more. "You can call him no such thing. Well, Lucifer, yes. But boss, absolutely not. I would be okay if you didn't let him so much as slip in a song request."

I laugh politely at this and ignore Lucien all together. "Deal", I say even though all I want to do is use all my breath to rip Lucien apart. Yet, now is not the time. I have to keep some semblance of professionalism.

"Anyway, do you want to join us for a drink?" Cole interjects.

"Oh, thank you. I'm pretty exhausted from my flight so I think I'll head to bed but Lumi, you should join." I still don't dare to look at Lucien for fear that I won't be able to hold my anger back any longer.

"Yes, join us, Lumi. Tell me if you need anything at all, Melody. This has my e-mail and my international phone," she says while smoothly slipping me her business card.

"Great. Goodnight, Brooke, Cole, and Lumi." I say, purposefully leaving out Lucien's name. I head quickly to the server so I can pay my bill and get the hell out of here.

And when I'm finally settled and leave to head to my room, I pretend to not notice Lucien's eye burning on my back and especially ignore the nagging desire to look back.

CHAPTER TEN
Lucien

I stroll from my suite to Melody's room. I harassed Cole until he gave me her room number so I can give her an apology, which he witnessed with his own eyes last night is sorely needed. I gave her space yesterday as she must have been exhausted from her flight, but it's time to confront the little pink she-demon.

Today, I feel surprisingly light on my feet, although I'm not even sure why. Yesterday, I was my usual grumpy self, yet today is full of something... Ah, yes. That's it. A game. There is now a game afoot having Melody here. The woman literally kicked me out of her apartment with my pants barely zipped up *before* she knew who I was. When I confessed, in the form of a very expensive instrument, she never contacted me and blocked me when *I* contacted *her*. And now, in person, she has clarified without a doubt that she wants nothing to do with me. Of course I should leave her alone. But there is no damn way that is happening.

I approach her door and take a breath before knocking. It's time for me to bring my best moves.

"Merde, what's on your face?" I say when she cracks the door open. Okay, not my best start. But Melody is standing before me with black goop covering her face. I trace down the rest of her to understand what's happening, but instead can only notice that she is wrapped in a thin robe that clings to her curves. The opening exposes the tender slopes of her breasts that are clearly bra-free. She looks like a sexy bog monster and my cock finds it extremely confusing.

"Man, that sure provides a cold glimpse into your love life if a woman has never felt comfortable enough to do a face mask around you." She rolls her blue eyes, which are only more accentuated by this monster make-up she has on. "Why are you here and what do you want?" she asks. This is at least better than the slammed door in my face that I was preparing myself for.

"You know, when your boss comes looking for you, the professional response should be more polite."

"Nice try, Lucifer. Brooke stopped that one in its tracks. You lost your chance to be my actual boss, Mr. De la Roche Records." She says, walking to the bathroom, not inviting me in so I take it upon myself to do it for her. I close the door behind me and glance around. Her room is clean and dimly lit with candles that seem to be the source of the flowery and spicy smell that fills the room. Her bed is made, and she has two white paper stars glowing in each window. Apparently she decorated for the holidays despite it not being her home and it not being the holidays anymore.

"Did I walk in on a masturbation session or something? Why is the ambiance in here so sexy?"

She comes out of the bathroom with a clean face but a sour expression. "Again, you're really illuminating your cold heart. Candles aren't *sexy* to a lot of women, they're *cozy*."

"Well, if you're willing, I can show you some ways to never think of candles as anything but sexy again."

She rolls her eyes. "Let's make this clear really fast, I will never touch you again now that I know who you are. What are you even doing here?"

"I figured we should talk."

"Sure. It was one stupid night. We were wasted. We weren't especially nice to each other, even when we were getting naked. We didn't have sex, so I won't try to claim some pregnancy is your billionaire heir in 9 months. Am I forgetting anything?" she says cocking her head and looking up in an exaggerated gesture to symbolize thinking, "Oh yeah! You are a heartless asshole who thought he would swing his dick around and crush dreams so he could prove himself to daddy. Talk over. Get out."

I push down a laugh. She's infuriating but funny, I have to give her that. "You clearly considered the billionaire heir thing. Excellent choice not going with it. Paternity tests have kind of killed that whole industry."

She shakes her head in annoyance and goes to her closet to pull out a dress. It looks black and tight, and I admit I'm excited to see it on her.

"Listen, I realized your connection to De la Roche Records after we met. I had no idea, and if it means anything, I'm truly sorry. We've adjusted our business plan. We were bleeding out with indie artists that we couldn't give the proper attention to. You will do better with a smaller label, and I have no doubt you'll be snatched up by one soon."

"I have to get ready for the show," she says, this time with an even and commanding tone. "So, if that's all, then please leave."

I weigh my options. I want to tell her that sure, we weren't nice to each other, but we were fucking hot for each other. I want to tell her I'm actually kind of happy she's here, even if it means dodging her fury. I want to tell her I sent her the lute because I knew she would do awesome things with it and I haven't been able to stop wondering if she liked it.

"You also didn't have enough original music. Developing new

music requires a lot more resources that would have been a bad investment on our part," I say instead. Why the fuck can't I just shut up? I wanted to explain the logistics behind our choices, to prove that I had a rational reason and wasn't killing young artists dreams for the pleasure of it all. Yet, now it only sounds like I'm blaming her. Not to mention, it's not even the whole truth.

"Do you insist on standing there telling me all the reasons I suck, or will you let me finish getting ready for my show?" she asks glaring at me as she brings a comb through her light pink waves.

"Yeah, I'm sorry. I admit that wasn't my best apology. I'll keep trying though." I say softly, noticing the graceful line of her cheekbone as she pushes her hair away from her face with the comb. I wish I could just offer to fuck the forgiveness out of her. I would take on that task as if it was the most important job in the world and wouldn't slow down until she felt completely worshipped. Yet, I would be lucky at this point if I got a smile from her, let alone an orgasm. "And it was more than just a stupid night to me," I add before I can stop myself.

I see her face lighten the slightest at my apology, but her eyes still burn with resentment.

"Well, I guess I should go." I look back at her and take her face in as it glances at me, wondering if she only sees a monster. "I'll be at your show tonight. Look forward to it." I add before closing the door behind me.

CHAPTER ELEVEN
Lucien

"Give me the strongest drink the Finns have," I request to the server.

"Oh, be careful what you ask for," Brooke chimes in.

"Make it a double," I amend.

"The apology went over that well?" Cole asks with raised eyebrows.

I grunt instead of answer.

"Dude, it's a girl you barely know. I remember when you were told Steph was on a dating website and you *laughed*," Cole adds.

Yes, my ex who left me for the geriatric lottery ticket didn't even illicit the slightest reaction in me. I understood what I was getting into from the beginning when I started dating Steph. It was always transactional.

I needed to look steady and reliable in contrast to my father, who was forced to step down after he got caught cheating on his secretary girlfriend at a company Christmas party. Oh yeah, and with an intern. The board had decided the man's inability to keep it in his pants was a liability, so I've needed to be the opposite. Which isn't a problem considering I'm too damn busy with running a company. But to add extra assurance, that's where Steph came in.

She made it clear she wanted to marry wealthy, and I made it clear I needed someone on my arm while I took over De la Roche Records.

And I haven't even thought about being with someone in a different way. Yet here I am, frustrated as hell over this girl. With Melody, it feels much more complicated. All I know is that she's got something I want more of. Something I already felt addicted to after one brief encounter. Yet, she's not even willing to negotiate giving me more. And it's fucking infuriating.

I chalk it up to my competitiveness. Melody has unleashed my insatiable need for winning and is the first girl that has actually made it hard. That's got to be it.

"What did you do to her, anyway?" Brooke asks as the server sets a dark brown liquid in a snifter in front of me. That's cute that he assumes I'll sip it instead of shooting it back. Before he can leave, I throw the liquid to the back of my throat and order another with a beer.

"Well, let's see," I start. "I indirectly offered her a contract that would change her life forever, then tore it up later that week. That same day I crushed her dreams, I found her at a bar, took way too many shots, followed her up to her apartment and puked in her kitchen for about an hour," I see Brooke's face crinkle in mortification at my answer, but I'm not even done. "Oh! And then I waited a couple days before I revealed I was the bastard who stomped all over her dreams, just so she knew she had let the big bad wolf directly into her home the one night she was trying to escape me."

"Yeah," Brooke says, still grimacing. "Yeah, that's pretty bad."

"You didn't know who she was that night," Cole tries weakly to redeem me.

"It doesn't matter. I'm a bastard, and inevitably the world should treat me like one. It just so happens Melody is the first person who actually does. I deserve it, so I'm not sure why I'm even trying to be redeemed."

"Did you guys hook up?" Brooke asks straight-forwardly, clearly trying to understand the entirety of the situation.

"Me not being able to hold my liquor is apparently not a seductive quality for Mel," I say, using her nickname without her here only because I like how it feels on my lips.

Before I can get interrogated any further, a smooth voice drips down the wood walls and into my ears, spiking the hairs on my arm to attention. *Melody.* She has slinked her way to the stage and jumped immediately into her performance. It's a dramatic effect that works. The entire room quickly goes silent, making room for Melody's enormous voice. Eyes everywhere dart to her, transfixed. Especially mine.

"You weren't kidding. She's amazing," Brooke whispers.

"You think this song is for you, Luc?" Cole chimes in.

I was so distracted by her voice that I didn't realize what song she was singing, a cover of "You Don't Own Me". She's certainly mastered the feisty songs.

An old couple gets up to dance along with the music and she smiles at them. I get a flashback to me on her couch playing for her, when I was on the receiving end of that smile and how good it felt. Her small encouragement bleeds out into the crowd and gets more people to get up and dance, in a way only a true performer can do.

"You let her go? I thought you're supposed to be good at your job," Brooke accuses me while still transfixed on Melody.

I shoot back my second brown snifter instead of responding.

Melody continues to sing, alternating between upbeat and slow songs. She has quickly transformed the ambience in this large room in the middle of the Arctic into something so much richer and intimate. For me, it's both pleasure and pain watching her. I am lucky to be this close to her, but I feel inappropriately jealous that I have to share her with all these people.

"You are a truly great crowd," Melody addresses the room for the first time. "My name is Melody and I'll be preforming here all week. I'm so happy to share this cold, beautiful corner of the world with you during this time." She pauses and twists the microphone in her hand before looking back up at the crowd. She continues speaking with a saccharine smile that can only mean trouble. "This next song is dedicated to someone in this room. He'll know who he is."

She strums her guitar.

"Uh oh," Brooke says, stifling a laugh. "This one is *definitely* for you."

Even I recognize the beginnings of this song. *Shania Twain.*

I stare at her, daring her to look back at me. If you're going to play this game, Mel, the least you can do is look me in the eye while you do it.

Then she does. She locks eyes with me as she sings.

"Oh-oh, you think you're special. Oh-oh, you think you're something else... Okay, so you're a billionaire." I hear Brooke's snorting laugh at this. Melody actually *changed* the lyrics.

"That don't impress me much," she sings with a sly smile. This damn woman.

Brooke is in a fit of laughter, while Cole is smiling too fucking wide.

I sit through the next chorus and slip in another drink order.

She changed the second chorus to, "Okay, so you're French." She continues, not even attempting to hide how much pleasure she is getting from singing about how unimpressed she is.

Finally, one more shot down my throat positions me into the third chorus. "Okay, so you own this hotel. That don't impress me much."

Brooke is straight up cheering at this point, and Melody is having way too much fun on the stage. In fact, everyone is having too much fun. It's a song that almost everyone knows the lyrics to, but when the chorus comes around they all quiet down to hear Melody's creative liberties, even if they don't understand them. This only emphasizes her saying how unimpressed she is with me to a room full of people. With Melody's direct gaze at me and Cole patting me on the back, I'm pretty sure not one person in the room has any confusion about who this song is about.

That's when I realize something. Melody resents me for the power she thinks I hold, but this only proves what I've known since I walked into that bar in Brooklyn. She is the one with all the power. She has a gift that gives her more leverage in this world than anything my family could hand over to me.

I know that should make me want to back down, even admit I'm not worthy of her, which I'm not. But that's not a fucking option. It feels too good to actually want something, someone, for the first time I can remember in too long.

So if she's mad at me for using my power on her, it's possible she can forgive me when she realizes she's the one who has much more power than I could ever dream of. And then, just maybe, I can finally have something in my life that's worth getting.

CHAPTER TWELVE
Melody

There is a euphoria that comes with preforming. It's only grown as I've become more experienced at it. At first my nerves were so overbearing it was hard to feel anything but nervousness. Now, it puts me into a state that I can't reach with anything else in my life. Even though my performance tonight was only for a few dozen people, it was an engaged crowd and that makes for almost ideal conditions. It would have been truly ideal if it were my own songs that I was singing.

Oh, and if Lucien wasn't in the crowd. Even though seeing his face when I sang about him was one of the more satisfying moments I've had in a long time.

I expect to slip away from the end of my performance unbothered, but Brooke has other plans.

"You're my superhero." She says slipping her arm through mine. "Seriously, I don't know why I wasted two hours watching Wonder Woman when I could have just gone to one of your shows and watch men being decimated in real life."

I let out a loud laugh at this. Partly because it's hilarious and partly because I'm relieved. "I'm so glad you're not mad. I know that's not exactly standard for a performance."

"Oh, please," she continues. "You've got free rein. We're lucky to have you. Not to mention, the guests were thoroughly entertained. As was I."

She's drags me to the table she's been at all night. It is filled with people that I haven't met yet. The only recognizable faces are Cole and, of course, Lucien.

"You up for a drink with us? My treat?" Brooke asks cheerily.

Before I answer, I note the table set-up. It's possible for me to sit in a way where I would face Cole and Brooke and not even see Lucien, who is in conversation with some pretty blonde girl, anyway.

"Yeah, sure," I agree after barely stopping myself from adding the clause, '*as long as Lucifer doesn't join us.*'

I lower myself into the chair, taking a deep breath to unwind as I always need to do after preforming. But when I hear a smooth French accent coming from next to me, I realize that relaxation isn't going to come quite yet.

In a few short seconds, Lucien has managed to end his conversation with the blonde, pull up a chair annoyingly close to me, and begin a loud conversation with Cole who is sitting next to Brooke.

I don't bother looking at him, as this is what he wants and because I hate how I immediately recognize his cologne which lingered on my sheets for days. I don't dare bring my nose any closer. I resent the treacherous hidden part of me in the pit of my core that lights up at the scent.

I open my mouth to say something, but before I can, Lucien interjects.

"I feel really lucky to have seen your entire set this time," he says, rushed and awkward while turning to face me. It takes me off-guard. The smooth and cocky man I've used for target practice in my brain all of a sudden reminds me of myself anytime someone asked me to read in front of the class in elementary school.

I see Brooke and Cole are clearly confused too. Both their heads cocked and eyebrows knitted, as if Lucien has begun speaking in Elvish.

And it almost makes me bring my guard down. Until I realize that's exactly what he wants. He's probably acting all flustered to get me to be nice to him. Nice try, Lucifer.

"Yeah, well, I hope my take on Shania Twain was *original* enough for you," I say, throwing back the word he used when explaining why his label dropped me- why *he* dropped me.

"I didn't say you weren't original, I..." he still sounds flustered, and I let myself look at him for the first time since sitting down. "Never mind. I'm sorry. I should just let you enjoy your night." A slight tinge of pink rushes across his cheeks. It makes his face even more striking, as if he's been exercising or other various strenuous activities that I can't think about right now. But is it actually from embarrassment? It's too difficult to believe that this man could ever be embarrassed.

"I'm glad you liked the set," my subconscious speaks for me. It's a gut reaction. I can't stand to see a person embarrassed. I would do it for anyone, apparently even the devil himself. "Maybe you can get up there yourself one of these nights and give another performance," I add.

"Excuse me, *another* performance?" Brooke pitches in.

"Oh," Lucien starts. I can practically see his face transform, as if he just remembered there were other people in the room. "Yeah, a lot of whiskey was involved. Don't count on ever seeing it. Once in a lifetime occurrence, like that smelly flower that blooms in the jungle."

There's that flippant and cocky Lucien I expected

"He was good," I say realizing there is a fire here to be stoked that's not the one roaring in the fireplace. "Passionate about his performance, I would even say."

"Dude," Cole starts. "Are you having some kind of life crisis or psychotic break? Is the pressure all finally too much?"

Lucien brings his thumb and middle finger to his closed eyes and runs them to meet at the bridge of his nose, which makes him appear so... exhausted. He brings his hand down and looks up with a cocked eyebrow. "Honestly, it would explain a lot."

"Hey, guys!" Brooke says, "don't forget this is a *vacation*! Enjoy yourselves. Go to the spa, take a sauna, chase the Northern lights. Oh! And that reminds me, I've organized a car to take us cross-country skiing tomorrow. Melody, you in? You have the afternoon off, right?"

"Oh!" I pause, thinking about what I want. When's the next time I could cross-country ski in the Arctic? And it's not like I would even have to talk to Lucien with the others going. "Yeah, of course. I'd love to, thanks." I would really like to not notice the small smile this elicits from Lucien.

The small smile that makes me want him to touch me casually, the way he did in the bar when we first met, like we were old friends who might fuck one day. A palm on my back, just high enough to be appropriate but just low enough to make me think what it would be like even lower. A slow brush of hair behind my ear. All of these tender things passed between us in the first hours of meeting each other that we can never undo.

I would gladly wipe them from my brain and replace them with literally anything else. Give me the first thousand numbers of pi instead of knowing how Lucien's body feels on top of me, pinning me down. Add in the lyrics to every Weird Al Yankovic song instead of the distinct outline of his unfairly generous hard-on. I would even take a direct implant of the Sideways screenplay, a movie I truly despise for many reasons, if I could just disconnect his damn smell from whatever receptors in my brain they seem to be connected to that light up every time he's around.

But life is cruel and I can't do any of these things. Instead, I just think about all the other musicians just like me who got the horrible news the same day I did. Yes, this good smelling devil did that. He's a dream killer, and I'm practically made up of dreams. No amount of chemistry from one silly night can cover that up.

I take a deep breath, finally resolved to break away from him and say goodnight. I don't bother to look at the dream killer's face as I walk away to safety.

CHAPTER THIRTEEN
Lucien

I find myself, once again, lingering outside of Melody's door. This time, with much less vigor to see her. In fact, I feel kind of creepy being here. She clearly wants nothing to do with me. I got the picture last night when she barely spoke to me before leaving without a goodbye. And I don't blame her.

But I'm here on a specific mission, and after it's completed, I'll leave her be. Maybe even for the rest of my time here, though the idea of that is depressing.

I bring my hand up to knock, but before I can, I notice that I can hear two voices in the room. A primal bolt of envy twists in my stomach, even though I'm pretty sure it's just light chatter on the other side. Really, anyone sharing a room with Melody makes me more jealous than I would like to admit to myself. Mostly because they have the thing that I can't seem to get- her trust.

I finish my task of knocking, but with a little more bravado than I had originally intended.

I hear shuffling, the peephole cover sliding, and then a sigh.

"I can hear you in there seeing that it's me, Mel," I say at the peephole.

With this, she opens the door. "Shouldn't your hotel have better sound barriers?" she says with raised eyebrows. She only peaks her head through the cracked door, and this frustrates me more than it should. If I'm going to stay away from her as much as possible, then the times I'm with her should at least be filled with, well, *her*.

"Am I interrupting something?" I prod.

"Always," she says with a sweet, albeit sarcastic, smile. Hey, at least it's a smile.

"Fine," I run my hand through my hair. "I'll make this short. Brooke has an emergency she has to deal with at the hotel, and Cole realized he could spend the day at the spa instead of outside. So that leaves only you and me. I figured you wouldn't want to go with only me, so I came to give you a heads up."

"Oh," she says with what looks like the tiniest bit of disappointment. "Hold on." She opens up the door wider and I see it's Lumi from the reception desk in her room. This slightly calms the little, okay big, envy monster in my stomach.

"Lumi," Mel starts while walking towards Lumi who is sitting with a guitar in her lap. Okay, I guess I can follow her in. She didn't specifically invite me in, but she didn't close the door in my face. "Are you free to join us to go cross-country skiing today?" she asks Lumi who sees me and her eyes go big. In fact, it seems to be the only face she makes at me. I give her a small wave.

"Uh, no." She says looking between us, trying and likely failing to read what is going on between us. Join the club, Lumi. "I have a shift in…" she checks her watch. "Oh, well, look at that. I should go now. But you guys should still go. You can't miss the opportunity."

Lumi places the guitar on the bed and leaves in a hurry as if Melody had just asked her to join us in making fun of kittens instead of some nice vigorous physical activity.

"Did you tell her I'm some Disney villain or something?" I ask, turning back to Melody, who is shuffling to put something away.

"No, she gets nervous around authority. Don't worry. I'll make sure to tell her you don't have any."

I take a step toward, which makes her do this extremely unsubtle shoulder blocking kind of movement. She doesn't consider that she's like a little elf shuffling around with a giant peering over her should. I can see clearly what she's hiding.

The lute.

The lute I gave her.

The lute that I assumed she already sold off to the nearest pawn ship.

"You brought it?" I know the answer, but I ask anyway.

She drops her shoulders, resigning to being caught.

"I obviously didn't know you were going to be here," she blushes and I can't describe how delightful it is to witness those rosy cheeks again. That perfect shade of rose that matches her hair. It's so beautiful, I would paint my entire apartment the color if she would let me get close enough to match the paint sample. It means I still affect her. That even in the smallest way, she might care what I think. And that's enough to make me feel for the first time since last night that I might still have a chance.

"When I picked it out, I dreamed of talking to you about it. Of telling you what it means to me and my time in France. I dreamed of you making some badass medieval sounding cover to some song I never would have been able to figure out for myself." I can't help telling her. That little blush is getting to my senses. She probably doesn't care about what I was thinking about when I sent it to her. If anything, it reminds her of my connection to music, and therefore who I really am. A heartless heir who smashed her dreams.

But to my relief, anger doesn't flood her face. Instead, I spot the slightest smile dancing at her eyes. It's so small she could deny it. But I see it.

"Listen," I keep going while I'm ahead. "I came here to tell you about the others. But the van is still scheduled to leave in an hour. If you can't find anyone else, I would still love to join you. It's not like we can even talk while we're pushing through the snow in negative temperatures."

I watch her closely, knowing that reading her is a delicate science that requires strict attention to detail. I'm pretty sure I'm getting good signs in the slight release of her shoulders. If I was a betting man, I would give myself the green light to celebrate. She breathes out a small sigh. I think we got her, boys! Melody might just be in for at least an afternoon. But she's a tricky, unpredictable one and instead of clapping in joy I just stare at her, squinting slightly while she works hard to maintain what looks like a replica of the flat line emoji face that Barb always sends me.

Oh! Now she's opening her mouth. Body language is looking affirmative, with a small shrug.

"Yeah, fine. I'm not going to stop you from experiencing Finland while you're here. And you're right, it's not like we can talk."

The crowd in my head goes wild. We did it, boys! The celebration gets a little out of control in my head and I am definitely smiling too big to be appropriate for this scenario.

She's really trying hard to stay in the flat emoji face, but I notice her smile cracking through.

"Okay, okay!" she says smoothly instead of smiling. She moves her hands to signal for me to get out. "That doesn't mean you can stay here and watch me change. I'll meet you in the front in an hour."

Maybe not, Mel, but the cheering boys in my head are pretty sure this is one small step to being able to watch you change every day for the rest of our lives. What? Where did that come from? Calm down, boys.

CHAPTER FOURTEEN
Lucien

"People do this for *fun*?" Melody shakes the snow off her hat as we step into the front door of a red cabin. There was a sign pointing to this cabin, and it was the only thing we saw besides white on the trail for miles.

"I didn't know the inside of my nose could freeze. What if I can never smell again?" I blow at my hands, cupping my face, hoping it will thaw me out so one day I can at least breathe through my nose again.

"I felt the skin on my face freezing. I was picturing my face transforming into white walker skin the whole time," Mel says, blowing in her own hands.

Her cheeks are apple red and adorable, but I won't be the one to tell her that. "Merde," I say instead, bringing my face closer to examine her cheeks. "Your skin really is blue."

"No!" she looks genuinely terrified before I let out a grin, to which she responds by whipping her glove at me. "At least we didn't have to talk out there."

"Mm hm," I say skeptically, because I'm not so sure she seems to mind talking to me right now.

I open the second door for her, hoping I'm leading her into a cafe and we're not breaking and entering because let's be real, the sign in Finnish could have said, 'Don't come in unless you want us to tickle your feet!' for all I know.

To my relief, it's better than I could have imagined and, dare my French soul even say, *romantic*. There is a fire roaring in a large stone fireplace and scattered around the room are mismatched wooden tables. There are a few people spread throughout, drinking hot drinks and eating pastries. An older couple is behind a counter piled high with various types of baked goods, which must be the source of the intoxicating cardamom and cinnamon smell.

I look to Melody and can see she's doing that little smile suppressing face that she does now with me. Damn it, I don't want her to lose all her happiness because of me. I'll be the one who gives up smiling if that's what it takes. I'll tell her it makes me absolutely miserable when she smiles, and then she'll definitely smile all the time. She would probably even start smiling in her sleep.

"How's your Finnish," she whispers to me as we approach the counter.

"Oh, great. We'll be fine," I say before I can stop myself. Two feet tickles coming right up.

"Moi," the older woman behind the counter says.

"Moi," I say back. Good start so far.

The woman waits for me expectantly for the big reveal of my order, to which I very smoothly respond with pointing to what I want.

Melody is now looking at me with a cocked eyebrow and a smug smile, which is much better than the emoji face.

"Yes, Mel? What would you like so I can skillfully order for you?"

She looks back at the woman behind the counter. "Glögi ja korvapuusti, kiitos."

The woman responds without a blink of an eye, apparently unfazed that she is speaking to a literal savant of the Finnish language.

"Why are you staring at me like I just cured cancer?" Melody whisper-yells at me. "Lumi has been teaching me a little Finnish in exchange for guitar lessons and I literally only said 'mulled wine and cinnamon roll, thanks' and two of those words are written on the board."

"I'm allowed to be impressed. You can take a lot of things from me, Mel, but you can't take that."

She shrugs and I quickly use the opportunity to pay for her order.

"I don't need you to pay for me," she hisses at me. Really, she sounded like some kind of cat.

"I didn't say you did," I answer, grabbing our tray.

I, of course, lead us to the most romantic spot in the place, right next to the fireplace. If she wants her 'korvaavoomvoom' or whatever, she is going to have to come and get it.

She comes to pull her chair out, but before she can, a little boy in a bright yellow onesie snowsuit comes waddling in between her and the chair to beeline for the fireplace. The tiny dude must be all of 4 years old, and he's already showed me up once, when he embarrassingly passed me on the cross-country track. Now I can tell it's happening again when I see Mel's eyes grow big in admiration. Strike two, little guy, strike two. I have to admit, his resemblance to a baby Teletubby when he's walking makes the scene pretty adorable, but not adorable enough that I'm going to let him take her attention from what could be my one chance to ever have her alone again.

She finally sits down across from me and immediately works hard to bring her warm glowing smile for the little Teletubby back to her flat neutral face for me.

"I hate that you suppress your smile around me, Melody. It kills me. If that's your intention, congratulations, it's working," I say before I can stop myself.

She looks up at me in surprise.

"I-I didn't realize I did that so obviously," she stutters.

"I don't know if it's obvious, but I notice it."

She sighs at this and looks annoyed. Damn it, what did I say?.

"What do you want, Lucien? I don't get it. Why do you even care? Are you trying to get under my skin for sport? Is this your idea of a vacation activity?" She is removing her layers while she is talking.

"You really don't get it?" I knit my brows together in awe at the suggestion she hasn't figured out what I want. "You think I send hand-crafted instruments to all the girls who let me puke in their bathrooms? No, Melody. That's how I show love. It's the only way I'm any good at. I bought you a gift because you cracked me open that night and I would buy you every instrument on this earth if that meant I could keep getting to know you." *Merde*, what the hell is coming out of my mouth. Maybe Cole is right, and this is some kind of crisis I'm having.

It's out now, I can only sit back and see how Melody takes it. She takes a deep breath and then starts talking slowly.

"You didn't even think I was special enough to keep me as a musician on your label. Let alone, what? Date me? You think you want to *date* me?" Her voice is growing louder now and I see the little yellow gremlin out of the corner of my eye watching us from the fireplace in fascination.

"If you would let me take you out on a date then, hell yes, that's what I want," I say earnestly. Because I am fucking earnest about that, crazy or not. I can't deny it's what I want.

She rolls her eyes. "Sure, maybe you like the way I look. Or you like that you can keep me under your thumb being a powerful music executive. Maybe you even enjoy when I preform, but none of that makes me feel good. None of it. Because you're also the man who made me feel absolutely worthless when you threw away my contract like a used napkin. And that's how I see you every time I look at you, as someone who thinks I'm worthless." With this, she shoots down the rest of her drink and begins putting the layers back on that she's just taken off.

"Wait, just hold on," I say with more desperation in my voice than I would like. "Just stay right there. Please." I put my hand out at her as if she's a wildcat and I stand up, backing up to the register.

I quickly dash to the counter and get one more hot chocolate and one more of that spiced wine thing she was drinking, both for her, and put them in front of her like a peace offering. At least if she drinks both, it will give me some time.

"There's a study that found when a person experiences a gain in power, it creates temporary brain damage. And when a person holds power over a long period of time, it becomes permanent," I start, choosing my words carefully.

"Yeah, well, that tracks that you have brain damage," she says, drinking the spiced wine. She can take hits at me all she wants as long as she's still here.

"I haven't been in charge of La Roche Records for very long, so perhaps there's some hope yet. But, regardless, the study resonated with me. Because as soon as I sat in that chair in the highest office, I had to cut myself off from my emotions and, to me, that is like operating with a much smaller portion of my brain." I observe her reaction so far. At least I've caught her attention.

"So meeting you made me face what I had done. I realized that I have become so disconnected from the precise thing that I am supposed to be safeguarding… music. The most important thing to me in the entire world. And because I can't let myself fucking feel anything, I couldn't bring myself to face it. But I am now. And I'm trying to fix it."

Her face now turns from interested to skeptical. "How?"

Fair question.

"You might not think it's enough, but I've written every person e-mails detailing exactly why I thought La Roche Records wasn't the right fit for them and referring them to my contacts in the industry that might be," I unlock my phone to find an example. I'm slightly embarrassed for telling her this. I wasn't going to, but she needs to understand how significant meeting her has been for me and that if anything good comes out of this for these musicians, *she* did it, not me. She needs to understand that I don't see her as worthless. In fact, she feels like the most valuable thing that has happened to my life in a long time.

"Here, read for yourself," I hand her over my phone.

She takes it cautiously, but she takes it and that's more than I could have hoped for. I sit there taking her in across from me, the fire shimmering on her pink hair is ethereal. She looks like a snow queen from the books my grandma would read to me about fairies and wood nymphs.

Time passes like this and I'm perfectly content, sitting near the fire and just being close to Melody. Every once in a while she has me open the next e-mail, but other than that I just relax, and somehow I feel stiller than I have since before I took over De la Roche Records. I know that likely has something to do with Mel, too.

When she reaches the last one, I already mourn that our time is likely coming to an end. She hands me back my phone with a long sigh.

"It's definitely not something the jerk-face that I've created you to be in my head would do," she looks mournfully at the fire, as if she is sad to lose the imaginary jerk-face. I say fuck that guy. "Those e-mail were genuinely helpful and thoughtful."

"Aren't you going to ask where yours is?" I say, twisting my hat in my hand.

"No," she shakes her head quickly. "Because I already know. What you said back in my hotel room is right. I don't have enough original music. I have some, but I just… they're still in progress." She takes a deep sigh. "Fine, the actual truth is, I have trouble writing lyrics. If I could write a song about writing a song, then I would have so much material. But when it comes to writing about other parts of life, well, it's not so easy."

I smile softly at her. "It will come, I have no doubt. You're so passionate about the songs that you cover in a way that gives them their own life completely."

"You think so?"

I nod yes. "But that's not the reason I haven't written you an e-mail. I tried. That first day when I got to my office after having met you, I wrote about a dozen drafts."

She looks up at me, her big blue eyes really meeting mine.

"The only e-mails I could write were begging you to come back to our label, but I just kept feeling like I don't even deserve that."

A small smirk curls on the left side of her lips. "I *did* fantasize about making it big just to spite you."

I smile openly back at her. "You making it big would never be anything but good news to me, so sorry to ruin that plan."

She swallows hard at this and looks at me intensely, her vibrant eyes take me in as if I am a stranger. If I wasn't sure she still wanted to kill me, I might take the tenderness in her face as an invitation to do exactly what I've been dreaming of doing, taking her cheek in my palm and bringing her lips to mine.

She opens her mouth slightly to say something, but before she does, her eyes dart up and a finger pokes me from behind on my shoulder. The older man who works here is standing over us and now pointing to his wife, who is holding a phone and beckoning me over.

Confused, I stand and walk over, realizing that the place has completely cleared out except for Melody and I.

I take the phone apprehensively and put it to my ear.

"Uh, hello?"

"Lucien?!"

"Yeah?"

"Oh dear god, this is Lumi. From reception. Brooke has been trying to get in touch with you for hours and I called this place as it's the only place open on the trails. Are you guys okay? You're still with Melody?"

"Yeah," I answer with confusion. I have my phone on mute, but I didn't think that Brooke would need to reach me. "Yeah, we're together. We just took a break. We can head back if she needs to send the van for us now."

"Yeah, about that…" Lumi takes a deep breath. "You guys didn't happen to notice the huge storm outside?"

"Now that you mention it, it's a little empty here."

"Yeah, well, the van got stuck doing an aurora borealis viewing tour, which is a whole other nightmare. But the good news is, the place that you're at now rents cabins so if you put me back on the phone with them I can arrange for them to book you both one. Brooke agreed to cover the costs already for Melody, so tell her not to worry."

"Wait, are you serious, Lumi? Really? There is no other van you can send out here?"

I hear a rustling on the phone and murmuring in the background.

"Lucien?" Brooke says on the other side of the line, seemingly having just wrestled the phone from Lumi. "Are you really going to give my receptionist a hard time right now in the middle of a snowstorm emergency? Where the hell were you for the past hour? I will not risk sending someone out there to rescue you guys and them getting stranded, so get ready to get cozy there and let Lumi book this so I can get back to the real guests."

Brooke is in no-bullshit mode, a scary version of her indeed, but an effective one because I agree like a scorned little boy and actually apologize to her. I hand the phone over so Lumi can work her magical, mystical Finnish on our new host and walk resigned over to Melody.

She's sitting on the stone lip of the fireplace, warming her hands. She looks content and I savor the image.

On second thought, thank god for freezing snow storm weather that freezes my nostrils. As long as it means I get a little more of this.

CHAPTER FIFTEEN
Melody

The same woman from behind the counter leads us outside of the cafe to a small wood cabin among other similar buildings. We step inside and are greeted with a sparse but clean room that makes up the entirety of the cabin. A wood-burning stove lights up the wood-slatted walls with an orange glow.

One single room.

With one single bed.

"Uh, Lucien," I start. "Lumi explained we need two rooms, right?"

"Yeah, of course she must have," he says while unlocking his phone. "Hold on, let me…" he types something into his phone and holds it out to the woman.

Lucien holds up the number two along with whatever he's typed out. She shakes her head no, and holds up one finger. Well, that is pretty clear, language barrier or not.

He looks at me apologetically. "I can use our jackets and make a little bed on the floor. I'm not going to force you to share a bed with me."

I give him back a weak smile, because I don't know if I'm

honestly going to let him do that. The jerk Lucifer De la Roche would absolutely get that treatment and it would give me an enormous sense of satisfaction. But the fussed hair Lucien that has made himself appear again to me since that first time meeting him in the bar shouldn't have to sleep on the floor. Especially because we've already shared a bed once.

The woman signals for us to follow her and we do to a little structure next to the house. She opens the door and there is also a fire raging in here as well. But here, there are only wooden benches and buckets filled with water and some bars of soap sitting next to it. She begins explaining something in Finnish and we both look at her with hopelessly confused faces, but I get the gist. If we want to get clean, this is where it happens. This must be the famous Finnish sauna I've heard so much about. The one I was excited for until it seemingly meant that it would be my only way of cleaning myself.

She leads us back to the cottage and points to a big stack of wood. I guess that's our sole means of not freezing through the night. Then signals at a small structure the size of a closet. And that, I put together, is where we go to the bathroom. Well, at least there's privacy.

She turns to leave before lifting her hand up to signal there is one more thing. She takes Lucien's phone, types, and points to the cafe.

He gives her a thumbs up and then she's off into the night, back to the cafe through the horizontally falling snow. We hurry back into the warmth of the cabin and shut the door tight behind us.

"Well, this is certainly an immersive Finnish experience," I offer. I've been good at shutting him out, but I figure I should make it clear I don't have the energy to be at war with him for the entire night. Especially sharing this tiny space. And his peace offerings might have helped just a little. Okay, a lot. The man practically melted me with his words and his bashful little smiles. I don't understand how he can be both people. The soulless record executive and the one who can make my heart squeeze with only his words.

"While a little alone time with you is the only thing I've been wanting, I promise this isn't all some creepy ploy to get it," Lucien says unzipping his jacket and pulling up a stool next to the fire.

I smirk. "I never suspected that, but now I probably would if I didn't have dozens of worried texts from Lumi."

Speaking of, I check my phone to see if she has any input about this one-bed-in-a-cozy-rustic-cottage situation. If anything, I wonder if she and Brooke are the ones plotting behind the scenes.

Sure enough, there is a message from her.

Lumi: Glad you're safe. Sorry I could only get you guys one cottage. It looks like you and that handsome devil are going to have to try to stand each other for one night after all.

Mm hm, Lumi. I'm sure you are *truly* sorry. She's as bad as my little sister when it comes to these things.

I look to Lucien who is watching me with a small smile on his face. I swallow hard when my eyes meet his. How does he fit so perfectly in with this cabin already? He has stripped down to only a grey henley and athletic pants, and half of his face is glowing from the fire. His long legs look ridiculous for the large proportion of this cabin they take up while only sitting. Ugh, and that little smile. Why the hell is he being so nice to me while looking like that?

"So what on earth are we going to do for the rest of the night?" I move my eyes to the fire. I decide it's best not to allow for so many lingering stares like the one we just shared.

"Definitely not touch each other," he says with a mock stern face. "No touching in the most romantic setting I've probably ever been in my life."

I throw my knit hat at him. "No touching! Don't forget that I hate you!"

He stands up and slowly walks towards me. He doesn't stop at the distance that would be appropriate for two acquaintances. Nope, he smashes right through that space. The heat from the fire emanates from his skin and that stupid cologne wafts all over me. I try to hold my breath for safety.

"Mm," he says in a low voice, almost a whisper. "That's right. You *hate* me. Too bad." He leans close and I keep my breath held even more aggressively now, readying myself to feel his skin touch mine. Instead, he reaches past me and grabs two towels from the pile that has been left for us. "Well," he continues as I finally exhale. "Then we're just going to have to get naked and not touch each other. Not my first choice, but certainly not a terrible option."

"I'm not taking a sauna naked with you," I say sternly.

"Fine, well I'll be naked, you can wear a towel and be a stereotypical American not embracing the local customs."

"You think culture shaming me is going to work? Really?"

He shrugs as he slips off his shirt. "Worth a shot."

I keep my eyes expertly trained away from his now naked torso.

"I'll go when you're done," I say stubbornly.

"We're supposed to be at the cafe in about an hour. Why? No idea. I'm hoping for dinner." He slips off his pants now and is standing in his boxer briefs, his thick muscular thighs screaming at me to look at them. "Come on, Mel. I can wear a towel if you insist and you can wear one too, but you shouldn't miss out on a wood-burning sauna like this. I had one when we came up to check out the hotel construction, and I still dream about it. You'll love it."

I groan, because I know what I'm about to do. If it wasn't Lucien here, it would be something I'd have done already. I have no qualms about nudity. I only have qualms about nudity in a small box with Lucien. Well, screw that.

I strip down to nothing in a flash and run outside with nothing but my towel. The cold takes my breath away and my bare feet in the snow ache down to the bone. A few long strides later, though, I open the sauna door and am struck with the most delicious sweltering heat.

I hear Lucien laughing behind me. He comes in with a towel wrapped around his waist and carrying a few logs, his arms bulging as he does it. How did this city business man transition into a mountain man so seamlessly?

He opens the sauna oven door and throws wood into it, filling the room with a crackling sound. I climb up onto the lower bench and release my towel, letting the heat from the oven pulse over every bare inch of me. I refuse to be modest for him. He isn't looking there anyway, just my face.

"You keep surprising me, Mel." He removes his towel and I focus my eyes on the glowing stones with rapt attention, instead of the more glaring option of his naked and glistening body right in front of me. His huge body lumbers up the small steps and settles on the bench behind and slightly above mine.

We sit in silence, the steam crackling on the stones and the glow of the fire dancing all around us. The benches face a big window which looks out onto a white wall of snow. A strong sense of coziness overwhelms me and I take a deep breath through my nose, letting my entire body relax.

"You okay if I throw some more water on the rocks?" Lucien asks after a bit. "It will make it a lot hotter."

"Sure," I say a bit hesitantly because I can't imagine it getting any hotter in here.

The hiss of the water hitting the rocks unleashes in the tiny space first, followed by a burning, unbearable heat.

"Shit." I say panicked. But the heat doesn't seem to listen as it only grows and grows as the rocks continue to screech with steam passing through them.

"Shit!" I say with more urgency.

"Go outside and come back in if it's too hot for you," Lucien growls. He seems to be barely handling the heat himself. "That's how it's done."

He doesn't need to tell me twice. I open the door and book it outside expecting pain on the opposite spectrum, yet it doesn't come. The freezing air that was torture a few minutes ago is practically refreshing now. I am buck naked in a freezing snowstorm and I feel like I could trek through the snow.

I take a deep breath and just enjoy the…

Oh, actually, on second thought, it is freaking cold out here. The cold air has quickly broken through my barrier of sweat. Oh my god, my hair is frozen. *Well*, that didn't last long.

I hustle back into the sauna and see Lucien jump to a weird position.

"Ugh," he says nervously. "Um, are you going to sit down or what?" He says avoiding eye-contact while clutching his groin.

"What the hell is wrong with you?" I ask with my arms crossing my chest.

"What do you think is wrong with me? There is a huge window looking straight out onto your naked body jumping around in the snow glistening like your covered in oil. Please, just sit, it's really painful to have a hard-on in this heat."

I hide my smirk and lower slowly back to my bench.

"Isn't the most sacred rule of Finnish sauna that it's not about sex?" I ask. This is at least what the internet told me.

"This isn't about sex, this is about a subconscious physical reaction that is beyond my control. Can you tell me an embarrassing story or something? Anything to get that image of you out of my mind?" He actually sounds pained.

I don't answer, thinking.

"Seriously, I know you don't like me very much right now but

I'm begging you."

I pause a little longer before I decide to take mercy on him. "Well, I had a lisp when I was younger. Does that help?"

"Honestly, no, which I'm not sure what that says about me. But don't stop…"

I laugh, but continue. "Yeah, it was one of many reasons I was bullied pretty badly."

"Okay, that kills my boner." He says with audible relief. "What fucking assholes. Give me their names. I'll get them all fired from their jobs."

"I have no doubt you would enjoy doing that, but don't worry, little 11-year-old Melody took care of it herself by preforming System of a Down at the talent show."

"No," I can hear the smile in his voice. "Are you serious? What song?"

"Yup, I sang 'Aerials'." I say proudly. "My dad thought music would be a good way to help me be confident with my voice. So there was this guy, Ted, who was a tenant in one of the apartments that my parents leased out and my dad saw he had a bunch of guitars. He knocked some rent off for him to teach me. Little did they know he was a total Metalhead. I'm sure it was a pretty ridiculous image, the two of us up on the stage going crazy."

Lucien is now full belly laughing. "He joined you on stage? This story is giving me more joy than any Christmas I've ever had."

I smile big, remembering Ted. He had no idea how to talk to children or teach, but it didn't matter. He was my hero.

"Yeah, it was wild. I would love to thank Ted one day," I sigh nostalgically. "But that day I preformed, I saw the effect that music has. All of a sudden people were kind of nervous around me, as if I had some magical power they couldn't understand. And, well, that was *much* better than being bullied. I see it still after I play a set at a bar. People assume I am really cool and intimidating, little do they know I still have that little nervous girl inside me."

"Yeah, after seeing you preform I can understand that people are in awe of you. In fact, if I was at your school and in the crowd during that performance, it would have saved me a lot of time."

"How so?"

"You could have just broken my heart then, instead of 15 years later."

I'm glad he can't see my smile now.

"Oh, come on. You were definitely a cool guy. You probably wouldn't have even gone to the talent show."

"Oh, I was definitely a cool guy, but for all the wrong reasons. People were friends with me because they figured I might invite them to a concert or give them a signed copy of a CD. Which, well, I often did because it got me friends. Probably why it's hard for me to get away from transactional relationships even now."

With this, I move up to his level on the bench. I assume it's safe from boners now, but I certainly don't let my eyes wander down just in case.

"Was that the deal with your last girlfriend?"

"Oh, absolutely." He says, locking eyes with me. "It literally started with a handshake."

"Oof," I make a pained face.

"Yeah, but that was just what I learned from my dad. How to make friends, how to have girlfriends, how to be a son. Actually," he looks longingly out the sauna window. "That's what made *me* love music. It was a way to escape all of that. A good song is a reminder of what is amazing about humans, even after you've been treated like shit by them all day. "

We sit in silence for a little, because I honestly don't know what to say. I think about what kind of life that must have been. Sure, my parents have their flaws, but they are so full of love that they practically drown me in it. I mean, just look at my mom; she is dying for me to move back in with them at age 26, and I don't even doubt she still will when I'm 50. Who can Lucien count on in this world?

"Well," I offer. "If it makes you feel better, I don't want anything from you."

He breaks his gaze away from the window and looks at me head on. It's intoxicating, being so fully exposed and so close.

"That's too bad, Mel." He says with a wistful smile. "Because there is so much I want from you."

CHAPTER SIXTEEN
Lucien

Apparently it only takes an hour to go from being naked and covered with sweat with Melody, to being fully clothed and surrounded by people over the age of 80. Hunger was the driving force, finally making us finish our sauna session and head to the cafe at the time we were told to arrive. But if Mel hadn't suggested we leave, I might have stayed in there for days, withering away while talking to her in all our naked glory.

Although I must admit, I'm not against the vibe these old folks have going in here. Judging by the pile of skis outside, it looks like they all came in from nearby and are warming up with copious amounts of spiced wine and some brown liquor that I've managed to keep my distance from despite being offered about ten shots already. Right now most people are eating, but music is blasting and there are at least two couples who simply can't keep themselves from the dance floor. And by dance floor, I mean the little space between the tables. But all in all, these old people are going *hard.*

I glance across to Mel who has a big smile on her face watching the older couple dancing nearest to us. Her face has a flush of red from the sauna and her hair is still a little wet, leaving little translucent windows of wet white fabric on her thermal. I remember that skin, exposed and glistening not long ago, and I wonder if that's the last time I'll ever see her like that. I really hope not.

While I'm ogling her, apparently someone else in our midst has been plotting. Before I can intervene, she is being swept up to dance by a man who is very much not me.

I glare at the man. Sure, he's got about 50 years on me, but that just means he's going to get all of Melody's trust, deserving or not. The one thing I want more than anything, this dude has in a second. I stare resentfully at his kind eyes and adorably dated dance moves. How am I supposed to compete with that?

My answer comes tumbling in from the cold. Two men and a woman hurry in the door with snow still on their jackets, clutching instrument cases, apparently bringing live music to the festivities. They really know how to party in the middle of nowhere.

I scan the group over, wondering if they realize that I've just joined their band. Well, at least for one song. If this is the last night I ever get to spend with Melody like this, then I'm going to tell her how I feel in the only two languages I'm comfortable expressing myself, French and music. Sure, she'll have no idea what I'm saying or even that it's for her. But I'll know.

I also can't get that night in Brooklyn out of my head, even if it's a bit fuzzy. The way she looked at me when I sang for her is crystal clear and engrained in my memory forever. I want her to look at me like that again, her eyes dripping over every inch of me. I need her to be reminded that we have damn good chemistry and that I'm still that person. So I make my decision. It goes against every fiber of my being to make a move like this. I guess you don't act quite yourself when you're in a life crisis, which I've now confirmed is definitely the case.

I move quickly, grabbing three shots for the newcomers. I lay them out in front of them and then point to one man's guitar case.

They get the idea and nod that I can take the guitar before happily sitting down with their shots.

I find a stool and get comfortable with the instrument, strumming it to myself to tune it while the music from the speakers is still playing. I try not to think about the fact that Melody hasn't seemingly even noticed my absence.

I know exactly what I'm going to play. It's the song that came to my mind when I first saw her singing in Brooklyn. When I was pulled into her vortex, never successfully making it back out.

It's an old song but it means a lot to me. You see, while Melody was fan-girling over heavy metal at age eleven, I'm not ashamed to admit I could be found shedding a tear over sad French romances at the same age. I practice the first chords of a song from one of these romances.

Our host sees me and gives me a little clap of excitement. She hurries over behind the bar and turns off the music. Eyes shift around in confusion until they see me, and the curious faces turn to observe me. The only one I am paying attention to though has a wild pink mane of hair and is now looking right at me. Well, now or never.

I swallow hard. I rarely play unless I am heavily intoxicated or alone, and right now I'm neither.

I strum the guitar. The room is small enough that the sound travels without a microphone. I can already feel the satisfaction of this decision before I even start. The emotion of being in this close proximity with Melody has been… a lot. This is a release that I can actually have, to make up for the other types of release that I can't with her.

I remove my gaze from Melody's so I can concentrate. I sing in the low and straightforward voice that the song calls for. The name of it is 'Le tourbillon de vie', which translates to 'The whirlwind of life'. It's about a man who is immediately taken by a woman when he hears her singing. They spend a night together but are separated simply by their lives, or the 'whirlwind of life'. They meet again and fall into the same passion, yet once again, life takes them away from each other. Finally, they connect one last time and don't let go, and instead tumble happily through the rest of their lives together.

I sing without any kind of performance, only highlighting the music. But I make sure that I meet Melody's eyes for the last verse. I'm happy to find that I have her rapt attention. Her hand is in the older man's hand and her arm lies on his shoulder, but her mind is with me. The intensity of her stare is palpable. Her bright eyes face me and her lips are slightly parted. I would do anything to kiss those lips right now.

Instead, I look right at her while I sing the lines that only I know the meaning of. It's intoxicating being able to look her in the eye and tell her a story that sounds a lot like ours, to suggest we might go through our lives together, interlaced.

I finish the song while holding her gaze and offer her a slight nod before lowering the guitar. The room claps for me, but I barely notice. The face on Melody's face is giving me the feedback I am much more interested in. I pace towards her and hold my hand out.

"May I have this dance?"

The man backs away and gives her space. A serious look hangs on her face as she looks to my hand and then at my face.

"There's no music?" She says in a way that sounds more like a resignation than a question.

"It will come," I say as I step closer and wrap my hand around her waist. She lifts her hands to mine and we step side to side. My heart races having her body pressed up against mine. *Finally*.

"That wasn't fair using French on me like that. You know how I reacted last time," she finally says, looking up at me with her face adorably twisted in disapproval. "What did the song mean?"

"It's a story. One I relate to," I say vaguely.

"Mm, so I take it you won't tell me this story?"

"Don't worry, all you need to know is that it's a happy ending," I say with a mischievous smile.

I hear a strum from a guitar, and a soft melancholic voice descends over the room. Apparently, the French aren't the only ones with a taste for tragedy in their art. I can't understand this song, but it does not sound happy. But it is beautiful.

I pull her in closer and I relish the feel of her curves against my abdomen. I hear her breath catch, making my blood run even hotter. There is no denying the spark between us as our bodies touch. It's something I was starting to believe that I was making up. But now that I have her in my arms again, nothing feels more true.

"The song was about what happens when two people refuse to let life get in the way of something real between them," I whisper into her ear.

"Hm," she says softly back. "Sounds unrealistic."

"You sure?" I ask as I look down at her face, which is now studying my own. And she doesn't have to say anything to me to give me my answer. Her face is filled with more confusion than me trying to order in Finnish.

I rub my thumb on the small of her back, assuring her she doesn't need to answer that question, assuring her I'll be right here while she figures it out.

CHAPTER SEVENTEEN
Melody

We close the door to the cabin behind us in a hurry. Even just the short walk back here was painful. The temperature feels like it dropped lower, if that's even possible. The fire has only embers remaining, and Lucien hurries to throw more wood in.

I take off my jacket, wrap myself in a big blanket, and plop myself down next to the wood-burning stove, watching the logs catch fire.

Lucien blows on his hands to warm himself up. I watch his body flex against his henley as he tightens his muscles in reaction to the cold. I think about how much easier it would be if he just wrapped himself around me like he did when we were dancing. How much heat we could generate together, rather than apart. *Get your mind out of the gutter*, I internally scold myself.

We're at the portion of the night that I've been wary of. Okay, and looking forward to in the tiniest way and absolutely in secret. There's nothing else in our world right now but the two of us, one bed, and this fire. And then there's the other fire, the one between us. I wanted to pretend it didn't exist, and perhaps I would have been able to if I never saw him ever again. But being this close to him all day has wrecked the defensive walls I've put up.

I hate that I want him. Just being in this room with him alone is intoxicating. Wherever his body is in relation to mine provides a warm tug, as if all the cells in my body are throwing a big party for just being close to him. The way he held me when we danced turned my cells into a damn rave. Techno music was playing, lights were flashing, and my body was *dancing*.

I'm sure it also had something to do with having just seen him serenade the room in French. That move was just unfair. He knew last time he did that it essentially melted my clothing off. It's almost impossible to see him as the big bad businessman when he pulls out a whimsical French song. Nope, all I could look at was the lush contrast of his sharp jaw with his soft lips and dark stubble, moving his tongue to make foreign sounds that were as charming as they were seductive.

He lowers himself down to the floor next to me, his face transfixed on the fire. I admire his strong profile and remember what it was like seeing it for the first time at the bar where we met. He drew me in because of his intensity, but kept me around because of his willingness to make himself vulnerable. Well, that and this inexplicable urge to get under his skin the same way he gets under mine. That hasn't gone away.

"You know," I start. "The night I met you, I was energized by you. Even though you were such a jerk. I was so happy to get swept up in a night of... well, ridiculousness, with you, that I remember thinking, 'Maybe this is the universe balancing things out for the shit day I've had'."

He turns his head toward me, the amber light of the fire dancing on one side of his face making him look like the most handsome devil in hell.

"Couldn't it still have been that?" He grabs my hand and holds it between his, warming it immediately.

"What you did, even if you didn't know me. It gutted me. When I saw you again here, of all places, all I could think of was how bad you made me feel," I say, trying to hold back a tremble in my voice.

"I only want to make you feel good," he says slowly and with a tone that is darker than he's used with me tonight. It hits me somewhere deep and primal, and I remember why I've been excited all night to be alone with him in the cabin. "I want to make you feel so fucking good you can't think of anything else again when you see me." The hunger written on his face makes my body ache for him.

I want that. I want to feel good. And it would so much easier if I could deny that I want him to be the one to do it, but it's just a big lie that has been exhausting to keep telling to myself all night. Every inch of my body *craves* him. When he finally pulled me into him to dance, that craving poured from the little place I had been hiding it.

He's just so close to me now, his soft lips and his intense stare engulf me.

My body takes control before my mind can stop myself.

I lean my face in to his, closing the short distance between us and press my mouth into his quickly, desperately.

He brings his hand to my cheek, leading my lips into slow, deep kisses. The warmth of his lips against mine trickles through every nerve in my body, lighting me on fire.

We're kissing.

We're finally kissing.

My heart races as the realization finally hits me. I've surrendered to him. And it is delicious. I inhale his scent and hot breath deeply, as if I can finally fully breath with him in my system.

His big hands wrap under my thighs and he effortlessly lifts me up onto his lap so I am straddling him. My body sparks being this close to him, wrapped around him.

"It's been torture having you so close and not being able to hold you," Lucien growls into my ear, sending goosebumps shooting down my skin.

"Your stupid cologne," I groan, "has been driving me crazy."

"Good to know," he says with a smirk, before his face grows serious. He levels his eyes down to mine and whispers. "*You* drive me crazy."

I freeze, unsure what to say so instead look deep into those eyes filled with promises of what he wants to do with me.

He leans forward, bringing me with him, and then gently lowers me to the ground, covering my body with his. He is so much bigger than me that, in this moment, it seems like he is the whole world. Endless miles of Lucien cover my body. He takes my mouth into his as he lowers his hips to mine and grinds achingly slow into me. My pleasure ignites with the sensation of his thick hardness rocking up against my core, even with our layers between us.

I take a deep breath, savoring the release of so much pent-up frustration releasing from my body with the thrill of having his hands on me. I move my own hands down his shoulders and over the ropes of his muscled arms. I bring them back up and run them down his spine. His muscles pull and contract as he moves his body on top of mine. Finally, I trace the waistband of his sports pants, dancing my fingertips across his warm skin and push across his taught stomach and under his pants. He grabs my hand before I can get there and interlaces his fingers with mine.

"Tonight is all about you," he says, brushing my cheek with his own. His stubble puts every one of my nerves on high alert.

He moves his body lower and lifts my shirt so my stomach is exposed. His lips kiss me gently on that bare, sensitive skin while his hand reaches to cup my breast. He easily finds the nipple through my bra and shirt and circles it with his thumb. I arch my back at the sensation that is already running hot through me. Lucien has occupied my mind for so long now and I've labeled the emotion pulsing through me as pure hate, even when it has often been lust and having him touch me this way is setting all of that free.

He hooks his thumbs into the waist of my leggings.

"May I?", he whispers while moving his dark eyes up to meet mine. Of course, leave it to him to be ridiculously sexy while having exemplary manners.

I hesitate before I answer. I could stop this all, move to the bed and make him sleep on the floor and never discuss this again. I could keep my viewpoint of him singular and uncomplicated. He's the bad guy and that would be all there is to it.

Except it wouldn't be true. It has never been that simple. If it were, then I would have stopped thinking about him the moment he left my apartment, and especially when I found out who he was. I've already crossed the line before this night. It's too late for me to ever go back to a time when I didn't burn for this man, with hatred and with lust.

I keep my eyes locked with his and nod my head 'yes'. I watch a smile dance across his eyes and his body relaxes slightly. I think a part of him was still expecting me to reject him, and it warms me to see he's relieved I'm letting him do whatever the hell he is about to do.

He begins to pull my leggings down and then gets on his knees to continue taking them off. He lingers there and takes my foot up to his shoulder, kneading deeply into it while letting his eyes wander across my body. My feet are sore from skiing and it feels great, but it also is a tease. I want more of him and I want it now.

Finally, he releases my foot and moves his body back over mine. He slides his hand over my bare legs, past my hips, and up under my shirt. I move to help him take my shirt off. When it's gone, he leans in to kiss me while he unhooks my bra and I wrestle to get his shirt off of him. I need his bare skin against mine. He sits up on his knees to finish the job and whips the shirt over his head. Finally, we're both bare in front of each other, the fire dancing across our skin.

"You're so fucking beautiful, Mel," his voice comes out low and hungry.

His taut muscles flex as he runs his hands all the way from my cheeks, over my breasts, and past my hips to my thighs. He pushes my legs open with finality, as if I have no choice but to surrender to him. And I do gladly. He lowers himself onto his arms and adjusts his position to move his entire body down. I admire the lines of his arms and back muscles accentuated by the fire as he kisses my stomach gently, moving lower and lower.

"What are you doing?" I ask breathlessly, even though I'm pretty sure I know exactly what he's doing.

"Making you feel good," he says.

I nod, a desperate surrender to him that, yes, I want him to make me feel good. I need him to.

He listens.

He brings thumb between my slit, moving it up and down slowly while keeping his eyes locked on me.

I can feel the wildness in my face looking back at him. He smirks, clearly seeing it too, before burying that delicious grin into me, laying his tongue flat against me and circling my most sensitive bundle of nerves. I throw my head back at the pleasure of having this ache in me finally being attended to.

He moves slowly and with purpose, magnifying every touch and letting me know he is in absolutely no hurry.

He brings his hand to my chest and rolls my nipples between his forefinger and thumb while continuing to lick me at an agonizingly slow speed.

Just when I think I'm going to explode from need, he brings his right hand down and slips two fingers inside me and starts pulsing. I moan at the sudden addition of pleasure and arch my back. I hear Lucien groan in response, apparently turned on by my reaction.

He removes his hand from inside me to take both of my thighs and throws them over his shoulders, leaving my own slickness smeared on my thigh. He changes his tempo and begins to devour me with speed and aggression. When he finally slides his finger back inside of me, I lose my body to him.

The burst of orgasm comes pulsing through me so intensely that I completely lose control. My legs are shaking around his head and hotness is pouring out of me.

"Lucien!" I hear myself shout. He groans in response and the gravel of his voice, muffled by my own sex, sends another shock wave through my body. He is holding my hips up against his mouth while I spasm again, not letting me escape his tongue. My body is pushed to the absolute limit of pleasure and I twist more and more violently until everything gives out and I melt back down to the ground.

Lucien kisses my stomach once more before moving next to me and gathering me up in his arms.

"How do you feel?," he says, rubbing his thumb back-and-forth right over my heart.

"Mm," I say, grinding my hips back into him. "I feel *good*."

I wake up to the cold on the tip of my nose that has started to make its way deeper into my bones. The cabin is cold. The fire has gone out while we are asleep, but Lucien is wrapped tightly around me. We eventually managed to get into bed together. His big arm is rested on my waist and his forearm trails up my stomach with his hand resting on my chest.

I can't believe the intimacy of this position. The man who I could barely look in the eye only yesterday has held me close to him all night, shared a bed with me, tasted me…

And what I really don't understand about all of it is… how it all feels so right? I was nervous I might wake up this morning regretting a temporary lapse of sanity, but I don't. I almost wished that I did, because it would certainly make everything easier.

Lucien, or Luc, as he insisted I call him last night after he insisted making someone scream in orgasm qualifies for a nickname basis, is still peacefully asleep.

I wonder if he'll regret things this morning in the light of day?

He takes a deep breath, as if disturbed, and I quickly pretend I'm still asleep to cover the fact that I was just watching him sleeping.

He gently lifts his arm off me.

Crap. The bare, cold skin left without his arm feels like rejection. He clearly is regretting whatever this is.

I sneak an eye barely open to see what is happening. He isn't actually pulling away from me, but turning his watch to him to check the time.

He drops his arm back on me and I shut my eye quickly right before I notice the warm press of his lips against my forehead.

"Wake up, beautiful," he whispers.

I summon the shamelessness to bring my best acting skills and pretend to wake up confused.

A part of me is terrified about how I look right now after one day in the freezing temperatures, a sauna, no face wash, and a rogue body lotion as my only skincare. Not to mention our dental care was limited to a travel size bottle of mouthwash split between the two of us.

But then the other part of me, which I'm attempting to hype up, identifies myself as nothing other than an orgasm goddess. Lucien worshipped my body last night, expecting nothing in return. It not only was physically amazing, but his unbridled lust towards me made me feel incredibly sexy.

So with that in mind, I open my eyes and do my best to keep that confidence going.

"Mm, good morning," I say with Oscar-worthy commitment.

"I love waking up next to you," he says, pulling my body in close to his.

"You're not so bad yourself," I say and mean it. There is a dim blue light that barely lights up the cabin from the sun that won't rise for another hour, but it's enough for me to enjoy the view as I trail my eyes down from the scruff on his chin to his bare chest. This moment is too good to be true.

"I'm only telling you this because you'll be mad if I don't. And I would rather say nothing and stay here all day, but, if we want to get a ride back to the hotel we have to ski back pretty soon."

And just like that, it's confirmed that it is, in fact, too good to be true. The thought of putting skis on and going back out into the cold is the biggest buzzkill possible. Yet, I have to perform tonight, and this fantasy world with "Luc" instead of "Lucien" can't last forever.

So I get out of the bubble of our warm bed and into the cold air of the cabin to ready myself to face reality.

CHAPTER EIGHTEEN
Lucien

"What the hell happened?" Cole asks while looking between Melody and I. She is on the stage with the slightest smile directed at me while she sings. I'm, of course, smiling hugely like a damn idiot. I've decided this is one of my favorite places in the entire world to be, watching Melody in her element and alive with the rush of preforming.

"What do you mean?" I say, not taking my eyes away from the pink-haired phenom.

"Well, Melody hasn't sung one angry song at you, you aren't scowling angrily taking shots, and unless I'm hallucinating, I think she's even *smiling* at you."

I run my hand through my hair. I don't want to jinx what this is. We woke up this morning to a freezing cabin and tightly wound up in each other's arms. I would have gladly stayed there for the rest of our time in Finland, or the decade, but I have no idea if she feels the same way. It's possible being locked together in the middle of nowhere caused a temporary lapse of sanity on her part. And sure, she hasn't been playing angry songs tonight, but she's not serenading me with the love ballads that maybe a small part of me was hoping for. She's chosen some more middle of the road songs like the Creedence Clearwater Revival cover she's doing now, which still sounds fucking perfect.

"Obviously, I have a thing for Melody," I finally answer.

"Ugh, yeah, that's like saying the sun is bright," Brooke chimes in.

I glare at her. "Well, Melody might have just warmed up a little bit to this sun then. That's all." I shrug.

"I'm happy for you," Brooke says with a smile. I know she means it. We've known each other since we were little and were both thrown into the cesspool of elite society. We're both supposed to behave and shut up and take over our father's businesses without a second of thinking for ourselves. And that's why I don't want Brooke, of all people, to view this as a happy ending when it's not. I don't want to give her even the slightest glimmer of hope that we might get a chance to be content, when I'm not so sure we do.

"Don't be," I answer. "I'm pretty sure she still despises me."

"Even after the dozens of lilies you had sent to her room?" She asks with a cocked eyebrow.

Crap. I should have known that wouldn't slip by Brooke in her own hotel. I wonder if she noticed how the shade of pink matches Melody's hair perfectly. It took a ridiculously long time to find those, and sure, I'm the slightest bit proud of it.

I give her a non-committal shrug and catch Cole's eyes burning through me in disbelief, most likely trying to reconcile the asshole he knows with the man he is witnessing right now.

"For the record, the two of you make perfect sense to me," Brooke continues. The woman really isn't letting me be mysterious and non-committal. "Since we were little, you've been one of the most passionate people I've ever known. But for some reason, as you got older, you seemed to consider that passion a liability. Which, sure, I get it. But Melody matches your passion, and I've been enjoying seeing you forced to admit to yours, just to keep up with her.”

This time, I look at Brooke. It means tearing my eyes away from Melody’s rendition of ‘Have You Ever Seen the Rain’ and that hurts, but this is important. It’s the kind of observation that can make all the difference in someone’s life, because as blinded as I am by my lust and curiosity and awe of Melody, I believe there is something bigger and deeper there. And this tells me I might not be completely delusional.

“Thanks Brooke,” I say, meeting her eyes. And I know that this is enough for her to know I truly mean it.

She smiles, self-satisfied, and begins clapping as Melody finishes out her final note. I join, relishing the opportunity to celebrate her in this way. I would clap for her constantly, but when I join the timing of everyone else, it’s suddenly not weird.

Melody thanks the audience and does a nervous little curtsy and then laughs at herself, her cheeks growing red. I notice her look nervously at me and I give her a big grin, assuring her that her awkwardness hasn’t gone unnoticed by me and she better believe I will tease her for it.

She steps down from the stage and glides our way, nodding and thanking the people praising her along the way. She is wearing a deep emerald velvet dress that is high-necked and long-sleeved but hugs her body like my boxers do every time she gets close. Her hair is loosely tied up and all I want to do is dig my fingers into the back of her hair and pull her in for a kiss.

Instead, I sit back while she greets Brooke with a hug. I get up to greet her. While I’m ready to give her a kiss, she is giving me a side-arm-half-hug and our coordination is so off that I basically chin-butt her head.

“Oh,” she says, bringing her hand to her head. “Hello to you, too.”

"We can practice that," I assure her.

She gives Cole a pat on the shoulder as a hello, and I'm relieved he at least doesn't get a side-arm hug, but I also have to marvel at how awkward Melody is being. It's kind of adorable. One second she's captivating every eye in the room, and now she is bright red and can barely look at me. She sits herself down at the empty chair between Cole and I.

"Amazing set, Melody," Cole says looking between us. I swear this is like he's stumbled upon ancient alien writing and he is trying to figure it out. He is genuinely perplexed by the drastically different dynamic between Mel and I.

"You blow me away every time," Brooke agrees.

"Oh, wow. Thank you guys," Melody says. "It just happens to be the only thing I'm good at."

"That's not true," I say a bit too defensively. I'm not sure even what I am referring to. She was a shit cross-country skier, just like me. "You're excellent at holding your liquor. Much better than me." I lamely try to save myself.

"Mm, well on that note. Why don't we grab us all a round of drinks?" Brooke says, looking at me clearly indicating she knows she's trying to save this fragile, delicate thing between Melody and I before we trample on it with our awkwardness.

Cole stands and walks away, still looking at us both perplexed. Brooke grabs his elbow and tugs at him until he finally takes his eyes off of us.

"Hi," I say softly, taking her hand under the table.

"Hi," she says with a laugh.

"I'm sorry if you didn't want me to come see you play tonight," I start. "It's just that you're the best show in town. I can't stay away."

"Mm," she smiles. "I'll pretend for just this moment that I'm not the *only* show in town. Oh, and thanks for the flowers, by the way. I gotta say, it is quite a spectacle in my room. It practically looks like lilies are growing out of the walls."

I notice myself tapping my foot nervously. The idea seemed perfect this morning, but now I realize it might have come off a little strong. "Was it too much?" I ask with a pained face. "Be honest."

She looks me in the eye now. She has a laugh dancing in her eyes. "You know, if *anyone* else sent me four dozen lilies perfectly matching my hair…" *Yes*, she noticed that. "… I guess, I would be concerned by how strong they're coming on."

"Oh yeah? And since it's me?"

"It made me really happy," Melody says, her blue eyes flashing with vulnerability.

I squeeze her hand. "That's all I want."

I glance around us. I can see Brooke and Cole lingering at the bar, Brooke clearly debating giving us more time.

"Hey," I start. "Can I show you something?"

She agrees, and I lead her out of the lodge, draping my cashmere coat over her. She looks made to wear it, the lush fabric brushing against her long neck.

I lead her to the ATV reserved for the guests. She looks at me like I'm insane.

"It's a short distance. I promise I'm not taking you back to our little cabin in the middle of nowhere. As much as I would like that."

She laughs and nods, getting up on the ATV sideways to accommodate her dress. I hop on in front of her.

"Hold on," I say and relish the sensation of her small hands grasping around my waist in response.

CHAPTER NINETEEN
Lucien

I'm bringing Mel to the best part of this whole resort. Well, best thing after her. It's the feature that sold me on this investment with Brooke. They are glass igloos, meant for viewing the aurora borealis and being completely alone with nature and if you're lucky, the person you want to share it with.

Right now there is a cloud cover, so there is nothing to view, but that's not why I'm bringing Melody here. I booked this place as soon as we returned this morning. It was instinct, really. I didn't want to leave that sparse little cabin where it was only the two of us, so this is the next best thing.

I guide her inside by the hand and we're greeted by the warmth of a crackling fire. They must have just finished setting up in here according to my requests. I notice the bottle of champagne waiting for us as well.

"Is this where you've been staying?" Melody asks as she walks around the perimeter of the room.

"No. I reserved it when we got back this morning. Just in case you needed to remind you what happens between us when we're totally isolated from the rest of the world."

Melody laughs lightly. "You don't have to do all of this... The lute, the flowers, this. You could give me all those things and if I didn't like what I saw in you, I'd still run the other way."

"Oh? And if you do like what you see?"

"Then I theoretically would be naked pretty soon, despite the fact that I'm in a structure made completely of glass."

"Then I really hope you do like what you see."

"It would be easier if you were a little less covered up yourself."

"I can do that," I say with a grin so large it could break my face. "I can do that really quick so you better be ready."

With that, we're in a race to take off of our clothes. I sigh in relief when we're finally down to our underwear. This is the state nature intended me and her to be in together. After tasting her once, all my body can do is crave her ravenously. We should have been naked in bed together all day today, and I would mourn the time lost if I had any ability to feel something other than pure joy in this moment.

Melody is breathtaking, wearing a black lace bra and panties that accentuates the curve of her hips. Every time I think that I must have hit the limit of my need for her, that it's not possible for it to keep growing because it's already fucking gargantuan, I'm proven wrong by a wild and ragged expansion that breaks me open for her. I waste no time letting her know it. I bend down to pick her up and I throw her on the bed as she giggles.

I follow her, moving my body over hers. Her eyes are sapphire in this lighting and looking up at me with nervousness and exhilaration. We haven't kissed since we left the cottage this morning, so to have her lips in front of me and her soft body under me so suddenly is a rush of euphoria.

I bring my mouth to hers and her plush lips are like a damn finish line after running the New York City Marathon.

"I'm never going to go this long without kissing you ever again," I whisper. I'm surprised at my own voice saying it.

"Oh, yeah?" She says skeptically.

"Yes," I answer definitively.

"Be careful what you promise. Just our trips back to the states will mean not kissing for even longer."

"I'll book you on my flight. There. Done."

"Our work schedules alone will separate us longer."

"I'll cab, walk, fly to wherever you are for even only a minute to kiss you."

"I might go on another trip like this to preform somewhere."

"I'll come with you."

Now she is laughing. I don't know why, as I'm being completely serious.

"We'll see," she finally says.

"We will see. And I'll expect a big, fat apology when we're on our death beds in 75 years and you realize I was right," I say with a grin. I know this statement is all kinds of extra, but I fucking feel it so I said it.

She smiles, a dreamy look clouding her eyes. "How about we get through this trip first and then we can start talking dying together in old age?"

"Fine," I concede. "But let me give you another taste of what 100-year-old Melody Greco has to look forward to…" I move my kisses down her neck, mapping my route down before she places her hand on my head to stop me.

"Actually," she says as I look up at her in confusion. "I was hoping to return the favor. After all, I got a pretty excellent demonstration many times over last night. It's time I show you what old man Luc has to withstand without having a heart attack."

I'm not sure what gets me harder, her threatening to orgasm me to death or her calling me Luc. Before I can decide, she flips herself on top of me and spreads my legs so she can settle herself in between them.

"Mm, I have a feeling I already know how old man Luc is going to go and I support it 100%."

She laughs while slipping away my boxer briefs, which usually those two things together would not mean good news for me, but luckily this doesn't seem to be the case.

I watch her reaction. Because yes, I'm only a man, and I want her eyes to bulge at my size or say something like, 'Oh my gosh, Luc, I could never fit this inside me!', even though I know that's not Melody's style at all and we're not on a porn set as far as I know.

Instead, she looks at my raging erection that basically hasn't gone down since I first saw her in the lodge days ago. The most delicious, barely perceptible grin tugs at her lips. It's a grin that says she approves and that we're about to have a lot of fun together. And it makes me feel like the king of the goddamn world.

She runs her hands up my stomach and back down again to my hips. She looks incredible perched between my legs, her ass and thighs condensed on her heels making her looks like a delicious juicy pear. When she wraps her fingers around my shaft, it's too good to be true. We're actually doing this thing.

She runs her fists achingly slow over me as she lowers her head. She brings her lush lips to the tip of my mushroom head and lays a soft kiss on it, before sticking her tongue out and circling it. I throw my head back from the electricity that is sparking from the tip of her tongue to the rest of my body, knowing that if I watch her do it, I can't guarantee I won't finish immediately.

That's when I see it.

"Mel, stop!" I can't believe the words coming out of my mouth. "Quick, get your head up."

I can sense her gaze of confusion on me, but all I can do is point up. There is a small opening in the cloud cover and in it, a green and purple shimmering ribbon of light is visible.

"Holy crap!" she says bouncing down next to me. "Wow."

"I know," I say, taking her hand in mine.

We take the surreal image in with only the crackling fire as a backdrop.

"I never thought a guy stopping me from giving him a blowjob could feel so… romantic," Melody finally breaks the silence.

I laugh and squeeze her hand tighter. "And I've never been cock-blocked by nature before."

"Well, I'm glad I can be your first," she says, turning toward me with a grin. "I've got an idea." She pulls my hand and leads me off of the bed, pushing me up against the ledge where the glass structure begins. I brace my body by holding onto the ledge and she sinks down to her knees.

"Now neither of us has to miss a thing," she says, taking me back in her hands. "Now where were we?"

Santa Claus himself could fly over us right now and I would only want to see this image of her right now, on her knees, ready to take my cock in her mouth.

It takes about one nanosecond before I am fully hard again and she pushes me deep back into her throat, this time with more urgency. She bobs her head back and forth, and fuck the aurora borealis, this is nature's greatest vision. My pleasure is spiraling, but I don't want to get there, not yet.

"I need to come inside you," I growl, my hand brushing her cheek to stop. When she releases me, I take her shoulders and guide her up and turn us around. I coax her ass onto the ledge. I find my pants nearby and grab my wallet to get a condom. I roll it on and she pulls me close to her. I kiss her hard as I reach down between her legs, taking some of her slickness to rub my thumb around her clit.

I trail kisses down her neck, biting her earlobe along the way. I end at her nipple, taking it between my teeth and swirling my tongue. Melody moans and my cock twitches at her, begging to be inside her.

"I want you in me now," Melody agrees with my cock.

I bring my face to hers again and cradle her jaw in my hand as I kiss her deeply and line my body up with hers. I slide along her slit first until she brings her hand to guide me in. I thrust slightly and my tip pushes into her. We both inhale deeply and when I rock into her deeper she clenches around me. We both exhale in agonizing relief.

I pull back and look down, admiring her slickness covering half of my cock, and we both watch as I push in as deep as I can get. I groan at how perfectly I fill her. We fit like I knew we would, our bodies destined to be companions in pleasure to one another.

I grab her legs and wrap them around my waist as I move in her. I watch her body undulating as she takes every stroke. She is so perfect. We are so perfect like this.

I can't hold back much longer. It's not my most proud performance time, but I've waited too fucking long for this. I rub at her clit in an attempt to get her at my level.

Her hips squirm under my touch, and I feel her pulsing around me. She's getting there too. It's all over her face and the greedy pulls over of her body on my dick. My thrusts become more desperate.

"Luc!", Melody moans and she digs her fingernails into my lower back, drawing me even deeper into her. It's her using my name and her unbridled show of need for me that finally shatters me.

"Mel," I can barely speak, but I see she is right there with me. I release hard, pulsing into her until she begins shaking around me. I lower my head to her shoulder, spending every last drop into her in total ecstasy.

We fall into each other, and onto the bed, our bodies completely resigned.

My eyes adjust to the sky above us. Green and purple lights have now taken over the entire glass ceiling, as if trying to match how I feel right now.

"It's like being in heaven," Melody says, eyes wide, looking above us.

"It really is," I squeeze her hand, which I've taken in mine. But I'm not talking about the Northern Lights shining above us.

CHAPTER TWENTY
Melody

"Let me get this straight..." Lumi says while adjusting the strings on her guitar. "You're telling me you climaxed... *together*... and then when you looked up at the sky, the aurora was out?"

I nod my head with a bewildered face.

"I live here and that's certainly never happened to me, not even close," She says to me with wide eyes. "I mean, you should really tell Brooke about that so it can be used in their promotional material. Or the Finnish government, for that matter."

"I'm desperate for work, but I don't think I'm ready to be the face for aurora orgasming quite yet. But honestly, it was so majestic that I do feel a little selfish not spreading the word."

"Are you sure it was the aurora and not Lucien that made it so incredible?"

I sigh and strum the lute on my lap, the one that Lucien gave me and I brought here when I was sure I would never see him again.

"Yeah, that's what I thought," Lumi says, self-satisfied.

Lumi is here to practice for her accompaniment for my performance tonight. My time on stage is shorter tonight, as it's New Year's Eve and a DJ will start playing at 9PM. So I'll warm everyone up through dinner and then join in the festivities afterward.

Lucien made it absolutely clear this morning after we parted that I am his date to the party, even though that virtually means nothing as we are both planning to be there, regardless. Still, it's that kind of sentiment from him that I find sweet now that I'm fairly sure it's genuine. God, I *hope* it's genuine.

Tonight I decided I would play "Wild World" for him. He's done so much to put himself out there for me, this is a small way to show up for him. Even though it will only be him that understands the reference to the night we met. Okay, and sure, I might have been inspired to add a lot more love songs to my playlist. Let's see if I actually have the guts to play them, though.

"For the record," Lumi meets my eyes now. "I'm happy for you. I know you were hesitant about whether you could trust him, but I think he's a good guy. He was super nice to all the staff here *before* he knew you were going to be here and could possibly get in your pants. How someone treats staff when nobody is looking is basically like a crystal ball into someone's inner-psyche."

"Yeah, as someone who has worked many service jobs, I can see your reasoning."

"Also, I can't wait to visit you guys in your Manhattan penthouse. I can even babysit the dozens of babies you're going to have."

"Okay, okay, that guitar won't tune itself," I say, getting up before she can see my cheeks go red. "And it's time for me to get dressed."

I finish getting ready for the evening, settling on a deep blue wrap dress that has stars and constellations sewn into it in gold by my sister. Lumi insisted I wear it and picked out gold drop earrings to go along with it. I love having her around for stuff like this. She's basically been like my roommate on this trip. Well, when I've managed to actually be here. I'm going to miss her when I leave.

We head to the door, Lumi helping me to carry my instruments and equipment. Just as I am about to open it, I hear a knock. I swing the door open and Lucien is waiting for me on the other side. He looks like an old-time movie star, wearing a deep blue suit and a white shirt open at the top, which perfectly frames his tanned Adam's apple and strong neck. His dark hair is pushed back sleekly and his face has a delicious half-smile on it.

"Good Evening, ladies. I came here to accompany my date for the evening," Lucien outstretches his hand to take mine. "You look absolutely gorgeous, Mel."

I giggle, yes *giggle*, like a middle schooler whose crush just talked to her.

"Lucien, I'm not your date for another," I check my phone, "hour and a half when my set is done."

"Oh, Mel," he says, interlacing his fingers through mine. "Haven't you realized yet that your always my date? No matter what time of the day."

"Oh my god," Lumi says, pushing past us. "You guys are cute but also a painful reminder that I don't have a New Year's date."

Lucien offers his other arm to Lumi. She glances up to me and I'm smiling, so she takes up his offer, a nanosecond of barely perceptible girl-code playing out. The truth is, I like that Lucien is comfortable with other girls like Lumi and Brooke. I know he has a sister, and maybe this is part of it, but to me it's that slight European slant I sense from him that I find immensely attractive. It's like he doesn't need to be so macho in a way that he wouldn't be able to be friends with girls. He doesn't have to prove he only likes beer and boobs to be a man. And after the delicious night spent with him last night, I can certainly attest that there is no manhood in question.

"If it makes you feel any better," Lucien starts as we stroll down the hotel hallway. "This is the first year I've ever had a date on New

Year's Eve that I'm actually looking forward to."

"Mm, that might explain why you're an hour and a half early for this one," Lumi eyes us with a grin.

"Damn, I just realize you're both carrying equipment. I should probably be helping with that, huh?"

"Oh, yeah, what the hell," I say, handing him the lute case.

"Yeah, seriously," Lumi hands him the guitar case.

I offer Lumi my arm which she slips her hand through and Lucien follows behind. I look back to see if he minds, but he just shoots me a smile. I feel a little bad, but I guess I'm still testing him, seeing how far I can push a hotshot like him. I try not to worry that one day I'll find his limit.

Once I get up on the stage, I'm in my zone. The songs pour out of me. I let them say what I'm not so good at saying without the help of music. Songs have always been my emotional crutch. When I was younger, it would get me through the bad days when I was bullied. When I grew older, the tool still served a purpose. You name it and it's caused me to sing. Once, I watched a documentary about all the animals dying and I was so sad that the only way I could muster myself up to go to the grocery store was to cover the 'Free Willy' soundtrack.

Yet, now I'm singing from a very different place. A place that feels a lot like love. There are so many love songs I enjoy covering, but they've never come from a place that felt true to my life. Yet, now, when I'm singing "I Wanna Dance with Somebody" and "Addicted to Love", it is suddenly like a channel has opened up for all this stuff I've been overwhelmed by. And it feels *fantastic*. Almost as good as it feels to have Lucien staring at me all night like he's ready to sweep me off the stage and devour me right there in front of everyone.

When I bring out the lute, he smiles so big I think his cheeks might freeze in that position. How can he wear his heart on his sleeve so quickly? I envy it.

I play my rendition of 'Wild World', and when I finish, Lucien's reaction is a little out of proportion. The man is giving me a standing ovation and forcing Brooke and Cole to their feet as well.

Before they can get too out of control, I introduce Lumi for our big moment that we've been practicing. It's my first time blending the sounds of the lute and the guitar together, and I really hope it works.

Lumi glides onto the stage, wearing a white ruffly dress, shiny plum tights, and silver heels. There is no trace of the prim and mollifying front-desk receptionist anymore. Nope, this girl is strutting and made to be on a stage. I smile in pride. If this song works right now, it's going to *really* work. If I do say so myself.

Lumi strums the guitar, hitting the low notes of the song. I sing the first line of "You Sexy Thing", the 70s era hit by Hot Chocolate.

The crowd cheers in excitement, recognizing the song immediately. I continue with the first verse. It's a timeless song and our version is definitely different, but it seems to get everyone excited.

People pour onto the dance floor and I grin at Lumi, who is smiling back at me.

It's her turn to sing her part of the song now, and she kills it. We bob our head along with the beat and sing our hearts out. The entire room is eating it up. I realize this could be a life-defining moment for Lumi, as it's her first time preforming for a crowd. The rush of making people feel things through music is addictive and I'm happy to be here with her for her first hit of it.

When we wrap up the song, I thank everyone and get ready to head off the stage, but they don't stop clapping. A soft chant starts and I realize they're requesting an encore. Lumi's face goes from euphoric to anxious. She shuffles toward me.

"I don't know any other songs well enough, Mel," she is twisting her hair on her finger nervously.

"You sure? Nothing else you would be comfortable preforming?"

She shakes her head wildly back and forth, in a very clear 'no'. I pat her on the shoulder, "It's okay. We didn't plan for them to like it so much that we would need a second song. Next time, we'll be ready."

She smiles at me apologetically and practically runs off the stage.

"Let's give it up for Lumi!" I shout and some people boo at her leaving, but the majority of people clap. Now I just have to figure out what the hell I'm going to sing.

"Alright, one last song…" Now is my time to figure out what the hell I'm going to sing. I look to Lucien, who is still clapping. Could this be the moment I find his limit?

"For this last song, let's give a warm welcome to the one and only… Lucien De la Roche."

His eyes get big and he shakes his head no. Luckily, I have Cole on my side for this one. He's already dragging him to the stage. Finally, he shakes Cole off, hands him his suit jacket and strolls up to me coolly, looking as elegant and composed as ever.

"Nice play, Mel," he whispers in my ear while rolling up his shirt.

"Just keeping you on your toes," I say with as innocent of a smile that I can muster. "I'll let you choose the song."

He cocks an eyebrow. "Easy," he says, grabbing the guitar.

I grab the other microphone, ready for anything as he clearly has no intention of informing me of what he's choosing.

Then he plays what is probably one of the most recognizable beginnings to a song. A song that he is positive that I know. The song where I first spotted his eyes burning through me. It's the song from the night when I was looking to escape a man I hadn't met yet but instead, fell right into his arms.

I look to him, and he isn't smiling, he's just watching me. I realize then I'm not the only one testing him. He wants to see if I'm truly over the anger that he saw in me that night. And to be honest, I don't know if I am.

The crowd is clapping along with the beat of 'Seven Nation Army' and I join them by stomping my feet.

Lucien sings first, his smooth voice carrying the words to the excited crowd. He's a great performer, even if he never normally does it. It's not because his voice is perfect, even though it is strong and damn sexy. But no, Lucien keeps eyes transfixed on him because he believes in the songs. I remember the extensive list of performances he sent me before I blocked him. The man might just be as obsessed with music as I am.

When he finishes his verse, he nods to me. My turn.

I channel all the anger, passion, and confusion that is brewing in me into my verse. In that moment, I know he realizes that all is not completely forgotten, and there is still a part of me who can never stop seeing him as De la Roche Records. Yet he looks at me with desire anyway and, well… that's the whole problem, isn't it?

CHAPTER TWENTY-ONE
Lucien

"I get it now," Cole says, looking proud of himself. "I get why Lucien, the cold, heartless shell of a man who you've become since you took over as CEO, is suddenly singing on stages like we're back in college."

"Oh, yeah?" I say into my snifter of scotch.

"Yeah, my guy. You're in love. I've never seen you in love. In college, I'd say you were in love with life. Then that all went away pretty quickly and now, you're blooming like a god damn spring flower."

I bring the snifter to my nose to smell the scent of the smoky top-shelf scotch. It reminds me of bad days at the office, a trusty band-aid for the gushing wound that is my life. A life that I don't see how something as pure and beautiful as Melody, as love, has a place for.

"What's going to happen when you get back to New York?" Cole asks the question that I've been avoiding asking Melody, asking *myself.*

"I'll keep seeing her, of course," I answer. But I know this is not the question he's asking. He's wondering if asshole Lucien will come back to the forefront, and if so, will Melody be at all interested anymore.

I see Melody, Brooke, and Lumi heading over our way with fresh drinks in their hands. They've created a little girl gang this week and frankly, they're a little intimidating all together.

I watch Melody throw her head back in laughter, practically tossing her champagne out of the flute. She is glowing tonight, well every night, but tonight she seems filled with a particularly potent brand of joy. I want to dream that it has something to do with me, but I can't let myself be too hopeful. Although, there is no mistaking she was looking right at me for some of those songs, and this time there were love songs. Sexy, luscious love songs out of her sexy, luscious lips. It took my breath away. But I know she's still wary of me. I saw it in her eyes when we were singing on stage together. I can understand it, too. I'll give her all the time she needs.

As the girls get close, I scoop Melody up under my arm and pull her close. This is our first time "dating" in public, and I'll use every chance I get to show the room she's mine.

"Oh!" Lumi exclaims and waves to someone behind us. "You remember Anja? Brooke and I invited her and her husband tonight as a thank you and so they can see the hotel."

I turn around to see who she is talking about, as I'm not sure there is anyone with that name I should explicitly "remember", like Lumi suggests. Yet, there she is, the woman who's little cafe and cabin led to Melody finally giving me a chance. I could run up and kiss the woman as a thank you for having the most perfectly isolated and romantic place in the entire universe the very moment I needed it. Instead, I decide it's more appropriate to nod my head in recognition and offer my hand.

"Good to see you again," Anja says in perfect English.

Melody and I crane our necks toward each other and I stifle a laugh seeing her face, a cocked eyebrow that probably matches my expression pretty closely.

"Wait, you speak English?" I finally ask.

"Of course," she says with what I swear is a wink at Brooke. "Almost all Finns speak great English."

"Oh," I say, unsure how to respond to this news.

"It looks like Finland has treated you well," Anja says, and she could be referring to the glowing smile plastered on my face or that fact that Melody is tucked under my arm. And either way she would be right.

"It truly has," I say giving Melody a squeeze. "Thank you again for your hospitality. You truly made it a night to never forget." I feel Melody smack my back and I grin even wider.

"You're welcome back anytime," she smiles. "Now where's this bar I've heard about?"

"Oh, please, let me take care of you both," Brooke offers and guides the couple to the bar, clearly ready to bring the party like they did on the night we spend with them.

"Were we bamboozled?" Melody whispers.

"How deep does this conspiracy go?" I respond, looking warily at Lumi and Cole.

"I don't know," Melody grabs my hand and tugs at it. "But we can figure it out on the dance floor."

The DJ is playing a very sexy Drake song that makes me agree to the dance floor but dream that we're somewhere else.

I pull Melody flat against me and feel our hips connect. I immediately get a flush of heat. My muscle memory screams at me, reminding me how well we fit together. As if I could forget.

"Suddenly, the New Year feels too far away," I whisper as I run my palm around her waist and pull her into me even closer. She drags her fingers from my arms up behind my neck.

"You know what I was thinking about today?" She whispers, a hint of mischief gleaming in her eye that tells me I'm going to like whatever she's about to say. "I haven't tried the pool once since we've been here."

"Oh, yeah?" I answer, trying to sound casual, even though in my mind I'm already ripping her clothes off to get her in the pool with me. "I bet we'd have it to ourselves if we decided we wanted to go for a quick dip before midnight."

She cocks her eyebrow and grabs my hand, wordlessly leading me off the dance floor.

The pool area is dimly lit and, more importantly, completely empty. As soon as the door closes, I pull Melody into me and kiss her with deep intensity. The heat of having her near is already coursing through my blood. I swear I am addicted to this woman. The scent of her, the feel of her, every time she has her eyes on me- it all sends me into a delirious single-minded need to have Melody as close as possible to me.

And to get even closer, we're going to have to get a lot more naked.

CHAPTER TWENTY-TWO
Melody

I've officially lost control. It is no longer the Melody that has always governed my life steering this ship now.

Nope.

An animalistic, lustful part of me I didn't know exists has started a mutiny and is the one in control. I've never been driven by so much desire for a person before. That's the only way to explain how I am, yet again, wrapped naked in Lucien's arms, this time in the hotel pool hall of all places. This need for him is as intoxicating as it is terrifying.

"I've got an idea," he whispers into my ear, sending goosebumps down my side. He laces his fingers through mine and leads me to a fogged glass door on the edge of the large open space.

As soon as we enter, our bodies are covered in drops of warm eucalyptus mist. A steam room. I've only ever been in one of these when I did a free trial at a fancy gym that I had no intention of joining.

This is much better than that gym though, because in front of me is Lucien's long muscled body shimmering from the steam that is slick on his skin. It's like we've entered a delicious smelling cloud together.

Lucien turns to me and grins. "You look like an angel."

"Really? Because it feels like I'm under the spell of the devil," I whisper, taking a step closer to him.

"Is that what this is?" He says while slipping his hands along my shoulder blades and down my spine, the water making his touch slip along my skin. "Because you're doing crazy things to me, Mel. I feel like I can't think straight."

"Mm," I agree. "But it feels so good to not think straight with you," I back him up to the white tiled bench until he has no choice but to sit down.

His head is level with my stomach and he looks up at me with a hungry and serious stare. He keeps his eyes locked with mine as his palms grab my ass and he pulls my stomach to his mouth. He kisses the soft landing of my belly, gently at first, but then lays his tongue flat and licks up the pearls of condensation.

"Fucking delicious," he grins.

I swallow hard. The lust for this man pulses in my every cell.

"I have an IUD and I've been tested," I say abruptly and with no tact. "If you want to…"

"I do," he says before letting me finish. "I want to so fucking badly. I've been tested too."

"We're, um, talking about the same thing, right? Like I'm suggesting we…" I don't know why I'm suddenly bashful, but I trail off without saying anything.

He cocks an eyebrow at me, amused. Instead of answering me, he brings his hand between my thighs and rubs two fingers along my clit, back and forth, back and forth, still watching me.

"What I'm suggesting, Melody," back and forth, "is that I guide you down onto my cock right here, right now," back and forth, "without a condom and we fuck the living daylights out of each other."

I swallow hard and all I can do is whisper a faint, "yes", as my breath is already hijacked by pleasure.

His eyes gleam at my answer, a smile crinkling at the edges. He's clearly enjoying seeing me reduced to a puddle before him.

He moves both his hands back behind me and does as he promised, pulling me into his lap. My knees balance on the tile bench on either side of his legs. His erection is thick and glistening below me. Lucien grabs hard on each ass cheek, guiding my hips up, and then down onto him.

We gasp as he enters me. I throw my head back, but he grabs me from the nape of my neck and makes me face him. I stare into his deep brown eyes as he bounces me up and down on his thickness. It's this kind of thing that makes him irresistible to me. He never touches me like it is anything less than sacred, paying intense attention to my pleasure and my comfort. But even more, he's not shy about what we are doing. He isn't hiding from the raw vulnerability of unleashing our lust on each other, and he isn't ashamed that he wants to fuck like animals. And I find the combination of these two attitudes to be the sexiest thing in the world.

He pulls me down, so he is completely inside me and then holds me there, flexing into me and letting me savor every inch of his skin connected with mine. I connect my lips to his, pushing my tongue into him, needing to be completely full of him. He wraps his arms around my waist and we stay this way, kissing one another wildly.

When we break apart, he lifts me up off him and with one quick movement twists me around so my back is facing him. He leans back against the tiled wall and then guides me back to sit on his cock, my legs falling on either side of his thick, muscled legs. He wraps his arms around my waist and chest and pulls me back against him while kissing down my neck.

He rocks his hips into me, sliding in and out from an unbearably delicious angle. He glides his right hand down as his legs spread, forcing my own wider. He brings his fingers to my clit and now Lucien is playing my body like a damn instrument.

I can't resist how he is making me feel. Tingling is creeping into every corner of my body and making its way to my core.

"Luc," I gasp. "I'm…"

"Come for me, Melody," his voice is dark and demanding in my ear.

I can't hold back anymore, the sound I release is raw and pleading. Lucien holds onto me tighter as I begin to quake around him.

His mouth still pressed into my ear pleads for me. "Oh god, Mel."

I love the way his body is reacting to mine as he swells inside me, pushing into me greedily. His hotness bursts inside me and intensifies my climax. He wraps his other arm around my waist and pushes one last time deep into my core before collapsing backwards, still holding onto me.

We sit wordlessly. All I can do is blankly stare at the ceiling, my mind turned to mush.

"Holy crap," Lucien finally says.

"Yeah," I agree.

We shuffle out of the room, finally noticing that it's hot as hell to still be in there, and slip into the much cooler pool.

Lucien corners me against the ledge of the pool, a hand to either side of my head. I wrap my legs around him, enjoying our weightless bodies brushing against each other.

"I'm so happy you gave me another chance, Melody," he says while looking me right in the eyes.

I look intensely back into his eyes, so unafraid to meet mine. I try to get all the answers I want from them, but I know that's not how this works. The only true answer is time. There is no crystal ball to tell me if he will ever transform back into the callous and emotionless executive that he described in the cafe. The one who hurt me and seems like a world away from the passionate "Luc" I've come to adore. Yet, right now, it is only Luc in front of me. So all I can do in this moment is answer him honestly.

"Right now, I'm really happy about it too."

CHAPTER TWENTY-THREE
Lucien

Melody is curled up into me when I wake up, the slope of her backside pressed against my front. We've stayed close to each other all night, even while sleeping. I look down at her peaceful face and am overwhelmed by a need to preserve this level of bliss forever.

Last night was one of the best nights of my life. Better than all the overly lavish vacations I've gone on. Better than big events like the Grammy's, full of celebrities. And certainly better than any night I've spent with girlfriends in the past. All seem faded and dusty compared to the vibrance of being with Mel and letting our need for each other completely take us over. It is hard for me to understand what exactly it is that makes my time with Mel so much better. The closest feeling I can recognize is one of peace, as if I've reached a destination after a long, treacherous journey.

After the pool last night, we dried off and joined the others for the midnight celebration. We didn't make it long until we snuck away to my room. Apparently a room packed with blooming lilies doesn't make for the most hospitable sleeping environment, and the glass igloo just seemed too far away in the moment. I'm glad we came here though because there was nothing here to distract us from each other last night. We had a chance to leisurely explore each other's bodies over and over without any of the shyness that laced through our first interactions. Like I said, a damn perfect night.

Mel's eyes blink open and quickly find me.

"You watching me sleep?" she says with a sleepy grin.

"Yes," I answer proudly and lower down to kiss her temple.

Her eyes suddenly shoot open in a panic. "What time is it?"

"Almost eleven."

"Oh, no!" she breaks away from me and sits up at the edge of the bed in a hurry. "My flight leaves in two hours. I have to go!"

"Mel," I grab her arm before she can get off the bed and lace my fingers through hers. "I already told you, you're flying home with me. I had Cole's secretary cancel the flight they booked for you. We leave here in about 4 hours, so plenty of time for breakfast in bed and whatever other activities in bed you might demand of me."

She tilts her head at me in what looks like confusion. "Luc, are you serious right now? You don't need to do these things for me."

I reach down to grab her legs and slide her across the bed on her ass, wrapping her back up in me, morning breath be damned.

"Oh, but I do. I need these four extra hours with you. I need your head on my shoulder on the plane. And I need to make sure you know I can't get enough of you, Mel, and I never will."

She smiles a small sly smile and then traces my chin with her thumb. "So what you're saying is… you're actually doing this for you?"

I flip her mischievous little self under me, onto her back, and bring my body down over her. "Oh, I think you'll quickly see the benefits yourself."

She giggles, and the sound runs down my spine and directly into my cock. I trace my lips down the smooth skin of her neck and keep going down, wasting no time proving just how efficient I can be with four hours.

The reality hits us hard when it's finally time to leave our little oasis of breakfast, sex, and each other. Mel had to tear herself away from me to make sure she could shower and pack before meeting me in the lobby to say our goodbyes. I smile, imagining her taking down her homemade Christmas stars and packing them back into her suitcase.

When I arrive in the lobby, she has Lumi in an airtight hug. I think I even see tears glistening in both their eyes. It should surprise me that there is so much emotion over leaving each other after only knowing each other for one week. Except, I have no ground to stand on. I would make an absolute fool of myself if someone made me say goodbye to Mel right now after this week together. I'm pretty sure Cole would have to carry me out kicking and screaming. It wouldn't be a pretty sight, and luckily no one has to see that because I get to walk out of here with Mel tucked under my arm.

I take the opportunity while they're still saying goodbye to leave a tip for the staff. They've all provided exemplary service on their first true week of work at the hotel, and I think the number I leave for them shows that and even more. After all, someone will have to clean up a room full of lilies left in Mel's room. Not to mention, the sex we've had all over this hotel, practically marking it as ours. Yeah, actually, they deserve even more, I realize as I pull out another wad of cash.

I walk back over to Mel, who now has Brooke wrapped in her arms.

"Thank you so much for trusting in me to be a part of your opening," Mel says as they separate.

"Are you kidding me? Thanks for gracing us with your presence. I'll be back in New York next week. Let's meet for lunch then. Maybe we can find a place that serves salmon soup."

"Mm, deal. I can't wait," Mel agrees.

I give Cole a fist bump and bring Brooke in for a hug when she's finished her goodbye.

"I'm really happy for you," Brooke adds before letting me go. "Mel is amazing and brings out a side of you I've really missed."

"Thanks, Brooke," I say as I pull away. "Hopefully, I manage not to fuck it all up."

She looks at me with a bit of concern, as if me suggesting that I might mess up is already admitting that I'm going to.

"You know you have control over that, don't you?" She says with a stern face.

I nod and laugh, as if I'm just joking. Yet, there's a feeling in the pit of my stomach that suggests that I don't actually understand that I'm the one in control. I push it down because the truth is too hard to swallow.

Because, if I'm not the one in control of my life, then I know who is.

The same person who has always loomed over my life like a shadow that chokes out the warmness of the sun.

The same person who's texts I've been avoiding all week.

My father.

CHAPTER TWENTY-FOUR
Melody

"I don't understand," I scan my eyes across the inside of the jet. "Where are all the other people?"

"The pilot is in the cockpit and Cindy is probably prepping a meal."

"This is not what I had in mind when you said you booked my transport," I say, hesitating in front of the airplane's door. The smooth cognac leather interior makes it seem like I'm about to enter a set for a music video. Come to think of it, I'm pretty sure I *have* seen this in a music video.

I was hesitant that Luc upgraded my flight at all, but reluctantly accepted it. But *this*?

"Listen," he says, bringing his arms around my waist and coaxes me in. "I realized that this way we could have more time alone together, before..." He pauses, clearly unsure how to finish that sentence.

"Before what?"

"Before the craziness of our lives greets us as soon as we land in New York," he shrugs. "No one was using it today, anyway. The company has it when we need to court artists."

Ah, the company. The subject we've managed to avoid with the grace and care of a tightrope walker.

"Then I'll leave it up to De la Roche Records to offset our carbon footprint, too," I say with an overly bright smile.

"I'll offset this trip ten times as long as it gets you to wipe from your memory that I just mentioned De la Roche Records," he says, pulling me onto his lap in one of the plush leather recliners.

"You know we can't avoid talking about the company you're the CEO of forever, right?"

"I know we can avoid talking about it for the next 8 hours, and that's enough for now."

I peer around. It will be hard when their logo is adorning everything from the headrests to the cocktail napkins, but I'll give it an honest try.

"8 more hours, then." I follow up with a kiss. He smells like aftershave. The delicious stubble that was growing longer and longer in Finland is now bare. I guess leaving Finland also means leaving behind that mountain man that was blossoming before my eyes. It's not like the clean-shaven business man has any trouble being the most absurdly attractive man I've laid my eyes on either. All these orgasms are somehow making him even more attractive to me, although I wouldn't have thought that was possible.

"Champagne?" A cheerful voice comes from behind me just in time for me to wonder if she saw Luc grind himself into me. I hop off to preserve some sense of decency and settle in to the chair next to him.

"Sure," we say at the same time. The woman, who must be Cindy, smiles and places flutes in front of us before seamlessly popping the cork off the champagne. The woman is gorgeous- blond and tan in a black dress suit. I can't help but wonder if her looks are no accident. I did some research on Luc's dad and there is no question that he likes women a whole lot. Especially young, blonde, curvy women. What does Luc think about that? There is so much I have to learn about him.

"Thanks, Cindy," Luc says with a smile before picking up his glass and turning toward me. It certainly helps that his emotional response to Cindy is as if she is a caring grandmother, not a gorgeous, blond, curvy sexpot. Oh man, I need to calm down and stop obsessing over how sexy the flight attendant is. Being envious of every beautiful woman around Luc is not the way I want to drive myself insane. There are so many other ways to go insane that would be much more fun.

"To a new year," he says, lifting his glass to mine.

"And to new beginnings," I add.

Before he can finish his sip, his phone vibrates on the table. He sets his glass down and checks it.

"Crap," he says, scrolling through something on his screen. "Ugh, I should take care of this on my laptop. It's an emergency at…" his speech slows down and his eyes begin to squint. "An emergency with Big Bird." He nods his head, as if agreeing with himself. "Yep, an emergency with Big Bird that I'll have to take care of on my laptop real quick. I'm so sorry."

"Mm-hmm," I say with a laugh. He is really committing to not talking about his work. "Okay, well you handle the emergency and afterwards, I really look forward to dissecting why Big Bird was the first thing to pop in your head."

"I promise I'll let you psychoanalyze me all you want," he brings his hand over my cheek and pulls me into a deep kiss before breaking away and slipping his laptop out of his backpack.

This actually gives me time to work on a song. I pull out my battered old notebook and favorite green pen and open up the page where I left off.

A nice bonus that has come out of this trip is that lyrics are coming to me. Not only coming to me, they are pouring out. And they are the type of lyrics that are surprising to even me. I've been trying to write for years but always have trouble finishing the song. I've tried to write about anger, sadness, grief, feeling inadequate, but this… this is uncharted territory. This is a *love* song. And sure, it might be inspired by Luc, but if he asks me, I'll deny it.

But as I sit here, sipping champagne and watching his 'serious face' as he types over the laptop, the butterflies in my stomach at least don't let me deny it to myself. Luc is my inspiration and more.

My first verse is about a sensation- the very moment I let my guard down and felt the rush of allowing myself to have what I really wanted. And what I wanted was Luc.

Under a Northern sky

I held my breath

With you nearby

But when you breathed out

I breathed in

Now I never want you off my skin

Now… what's the refrain? I let my eyes linger from Luc's furrowed brow to his soft red lips while the bubbles from the champagne tingle my nose. His phone vibrates, this time with a call. He looks at me apologetically and picks it up, walking to a bench at the other side of the cabin. He takes a seat to discuss with the caller but stares right at me. He watches me as I stare back at him. He looks so… expensive. His deep blue pants and grey cashmere sweater match the vibe of this private jet perfectly. His face has the symmetrical lines of his supermodel mother, but now it is stern, burdened with the weight of managing millions of dollars day to day. How is it possible that this is the man that has totally and completely taken my heart? I've never met a person more far removed from my world. He's removed from most people's version of the world, in an underworld all his own.

The devil was an angel

So the story goes

I write in my notebook. His eyes perk up when I look back at him, looking back and forth from me to the notebook, before he cocks his head in question. "Are you writing?" He mouths silently while strumming an imaginary guitar.

I laugh and nod yes.

He is an angel and a devil

But I'm in love with both

I write out some chords that seem like they would go well with the song and wish that I could take my guitar out to test them. But not while Luc is on a call that seems to go on forever. Cindy comes over and whispers to me that we're about to take off, so I fasten my seatbelt and Luc does the same from across the plane, mouthing 'sorry' again. Apparently, he is hooked up to Wi-Fi or private jets have different rules because he continues talking through take-off.

Once we're gliding through the dark sky, I put my headphones on for some inspiration and close my eyes, letting my looming tiredness take over me.

Eventually, Luc curls up next to me and falls asleep as well. We both slip in and out of consciousness throughout the flight. Any dreams of joining the mile-high club or enjoying the luxuriousness of a private jet are taken over by severe jet-lag, and sure, maybe the slightest desire to not *love* the jet. It's basically a trophy to wealth that I imagine a lot of insecure old dudes have enjoyed after building their empires on the backs of musicians. I wish I could stop myself from feeling that way, but the only thing I genuinely like it for is that it was an earnest attempt by Luc to make me happy. Okay, it's nice that I won't smell like 100 other people after a cross-Atlantic flight. I wonder when he's going to learn that he doesn't need to get me these kinds of things for me to like him. In fact, I might even like him more without them.

When we land, it is only 8 PM in New York but 3 AM in Finland and my body certainly feels that way. Luc's head rests on my shoulder and we're both curled up under the same blanket. I look at his dark eyelashes slashing through the peaceful slopes of his face and am struck by a tug of missing him already. At the very least, the New York City boroughs we each call home will separate us, but now that we're back to our real lives, who knows what else?

I stroke his hair softly to wake him. When that doesn't work, I kiss his forehead. He looks up at me blinking and confused, then seems to remember where he is and smiles the most adorable sleepy smile up at me. In this moment, he is nothing but pure angel.

We arrive through a separate part of the airport where we don't have to go through the normal immigration and customs lines. Okay, I guess a private jet has many advantages. But we still have to wait while they set up for us. I twirl my rings around my fingers, wondering what to say. I can't help but anticipate the point will finally come when we say goodbye. New York City is so big compared to our little world in the north. Couldn't we get sucked up into the city and never find our way back to each other again?

"Merde," Luc runs his hands through his hair, looking down at his phone. Right at that moment, one of the immigration officers waves me over. I look at Luc questioningly, wondering what's wrong.

"Ah, go ahead. I'll meet you on the other side," he says with a nod.

I walk up to the table to be inspected by an older gentleman with silver hair and a unimpressed face. I answer the obligatory questions, but am distracted, my eyes seeking Luc to make sure everything is okay.

"Miss," the immigration officer says with impatience. "Some place you'd rather be?"

"Oh, no," I bite my nail. "I'm sorry, I was just making sure my, uh, friend got through okay."

"You only need to be concerned with yourself right now."

"Of course," I nod. "I'm sorry."

I manage to get myself back into the country successfully without pissing off any more officers and see Luc already waiting for me.

He gets off the phone and paces toward me, looking distressed.

"That was my driver. He warned me that there was some kind of tip about me being here with a woman. I have no idea where they got it from, but they have been dying for a story like this since my break-up with…" He trails off, seemingly unwilling to even say her name.

"Oh, okay," I say, uncertain of what the appropriate response to this is. I'm sorry?

"I can't put you through this. They would stalk you online to figure out who you are, and it just would be all too much. I told my driver, Mark, to take you home and I've already ordered myself a cab."

"Oh, okay." I say yet again. This is really outside of my comfort zone, and I'm not doing a smooth job of hiding that.

"He'll be waiting for you as soon as you step outside those doors," Luc points to the doors and looks around anxiously.

"Oh…" I say looking to the door and back to him. "Okay." I'm really on a roll here with my responses.

This is the moment, I realize. This is the moment I've been dreading. Luc seems to want to keep a solid distance of 5 feet between us, as if getting too close to me on American soil will detonate an explosion.

"Alright," I finally say, realizing that he has no intention of kissing me goodbye. "Goodbye, then."

"I'm sorry," he says, looking around again, and back at the doors. "I don't know if they can see in here." The man who, just last night, made love to me in a place anyone could have walked in, now looks anxious to be seen only talking to me.

"I hate to leave you this way. Let's meet back up as soon as we get a good night sleep," he adds with finality.

"Yeah," I say, twisting my hand tight around my guitar case. I step to the door. "Thanks for the flight by the way." I say looking back, before turning away and walking through the doors, leaving Luc behind.

Flashes immediately start going off as soon as I exit, but stop as quickly as they started. Because of course they don't want pictures of me. I'm a nobody if Luc isn't by my side. It was my fear before I even let him into my heart, and now that fear has finally been confirmed.

CHAPTER TWENTY-FIVE
Lucien

It is slightly surreal being back in the white lines and shiny surfaces of De la Roche Records. It was only a week in Finland, but it feels like an entire lifetime. I have my feet up on my desk, and even though I have a million things to do, I'm sitting here and staring out the window. I guess this is what people would call... reflecting?

Barb knocks lightly as a warning and comes in with my coffee.

"You alright, Mr. De la Roche?" She is eyeing me warily, clearly not used to seeing me as anything but busy at the office. I notice she got the matching diamond earrings for her necklace, as she said she would after she got her Christmas bonus.

"Thanks, Barb. I'm fine. I was just thinking..." I dart my eyes back out the window. "Isn't it strange that this company is founded on one of the most inspiring art forms known to humanity, yet our office is like a damn laboratory?"

Deafening silence from Barb fills my office. I turn to look at her, genuinely wanting to hear her answer. Instead, she is just sort of blinking at me. Then resolve lines her face. "Oh, no... Did you do that drug thing that all the millennials are doing? Did you go to the desert and do ashwagandha or whatever it is?"

I laugh a full belly laugh. I can tell this reaction doesn't comfort her, but in fact seems to alarm her even more.

"Ayahuasca?" I ask when I finally compose myself.

"Yeah, I watched a special on that and, I don't know, whatever happened to just reading a book? Why does your generation have to do everything with drugs?"

I nod, eager to appease her. "Agreed, Barb. I promise, no drugs were present on my vacation unless you count oxytocin, which there was a lot of."

"Ah, the love drug. I don't need a special to know about that," Barb says, her hands going to her hips and suddenly looking like she can tell me anything and everything I need to learn. And I want her to. I need someone to tell me what the hell is going on with my brain, because this is not anything I've experienced before. It's like I've been hijacked by some invisible force where my sole purpose has now become to kiss Melody, and to talk to Melody, and to intertwine my body so deep into Melody that we melt into each other over and over.

And I would ask Barb everything, because I know she too has been similarly hijacked by her husband, Bob, and has remained that way even after 40 years. Even when Bob buys her a vacuum for Christmas. Even when Bob comes home, having completely forgot to buy the turkey on Thanksgiving. Even with a name like Bob. I can see she loves that man when her eyes light up when she talks about him. I suddenly feel like I could be on the precipice of having the same thing, despite it being a future I never imagined for myself in my wildest dreams. Well, not a future with Bob, no, but to go through life so deliciously hijacked that I want to spend it with another person.

And I would ask Barb every last detail if I didn't sense an acrid cloud coming my way. Yes, the cologne that told me as a kid to be on my "best behavior" before the source of the smell even got in the room. That cloud of doom is close, and it's attached to the very person who has made me doubt a happiness like Barb and Bob's could ever exist in my life.

"Hello, son," my father strolls in with an icy glare that suggests he is calling me son as a power move rather than a term of endearment.

And with that, Barb has made herself disappear. I don't blame her.

"Tell me, Dominick," I address him, cutting to the chase. "Was the destruction of any possibility to witness healthy examples of affection not enough interference in my love life? Now you need to send paparazzi to harass me with my dates?"

"A simple thank you will do. I'm trying to save this company while you're gone doing what exactly? Looking for Santa in Finland? Well, sorry son, Santa is a big lie. I guess I should have told you sooner."

I observe him and the entitled way he moves through my space, like it is his and I am only borrowing it. His silver hair is neatly cut, and he is freshly shaven, the same way it has been my entire life. Except he isn't maintaining it for the office anymore. No, only vanity. He lost his chance to be the ruler of this office, this company. Yet, he doesn't seem to understand that yet.

"You want a thank you?" I say, throttling my rage. "What exactly would you like me to thank you for? Reminding me *again* why I don't want to be like you?"

"For coming up with a perfect plan to save your ass. When reports get out that one of the musicians you cut from the label is dating you, the others will be discouraged to try to take you to court for breeching contract."

"How did you even know..." I stop before I finish that sentence. My use of the private jet probably tipped him off, and all he needed to get was Melody's passport information from the logs to figure out the rest. Damn it.

"You don't want to be the person who sinks De la Roche Records. It will ruin my legacy and turn you into a laughingstock. Another fallen angel of nepotism." He watches me with his hands in his suit-pant pockets, completely relaxed as if this is as normal as a father updating his son on the Yankee's score.

I don't bother to remind him it was his insistence that I cut so many of the young artists and that I've barely been able to run this place without him manipulating and controlling me at every turn. Because whatever bad happens, I'll get the blame and whatever good happens, he'll praise himself. Nothing I say will change that.

"I'm having a fundraiser on Friday," he continues. "I'm sending an invitation today to this Melody Greco girl. You will come together and it will be the official announcement that you're dating."

Melody isn't a fucking prop, I scream in my head. I've learned long ago to keep the 'tantrums' inside of me away from him. No, I have to hit him from a direction he can't see coming.

"Melody and I are no longer seeing each other," I say instead. "She won't come."

"What the hell did you do?" He sneers at me. "Whatever, I don't want to hear about it. Just fix it before Friday. I expect to see you both. *Together.*"

Over my dead body.

"I'll see what I can do," I lie.

I will fix it between Melody and I, but not the way he wants. I'll do what a part of me knew would always be the outcome of this brief moment of, whatever it is, with Melody. De la Roche's can have many things, but a 'happily ever after' has never been one of them.

CHAPTER TWENTY-SIX
Melody

"Hey, my darling sister?" Julia, my little sister, asks while splayed out on my couch. She seems to think that me being gone for a week is me relinquishing my rights to my apartment and handing it over to her.

"Uh oh," I answer while throwing my dirty laundry from the trip into a laundry bag. "That isn't a promising beginning. What do you want?"

She bats her eyelashes innocently. "I'm just wondering why the neighbor we all saw leaving from your apartment building is in a photo with you in Finland?"

Crap.

She is holding up her phone, which shows Cole's Instagram. The dude has hundreds of thousands of followers and tagged me in a photo from New Year's Eve. It's Brooke, Cole, Lumi, Luc, and I chatting near the fire, but Luc's arm is wrapped tightly around me. Luc doesn't have an Instagram, so luckily my sister won't know I'm cozy with the man I exclusively called the devil before going to Finland. No, as an older sister I have to inspire a little more self-respect in her than that.

But I can't hide from her the fact that this man is most definitely not my neighbor.

I move her legs and sit on the edge of the couch. "Well, Jules, sometimes when a man and a woman really like each other…" I start with a smirk.

She throws a pillow at me. "Melody! I'm 16! An adult! I just want you to talk to my like I'm a friend. And it's not like you're protecting me from some big and bad thing by not telling me about your love life."

"Oh, you're an adult, huh?" I say teasing, but I can see her face is serious. "Alright, I'm sorry. I don't mean to treat you like you're younger than you are, I just… I'm still figuring out a lot of this stuff too, so I don't want to be a bad influence."

She shrugs, "I don't want you to be an *influence*," she says the word in air quotes, "I just want you to be my sister. If we were closer in age, we would be figuring all this stuff out together anyway."

I put her legs on my lap and look at her. When did it happen that she is suddenly a young woman? Our parents had tried for a baby for so long after they had me. They had nearly given up, but then Julia came along, laughing and giggling into our family. I'm ten years older than her and often cared for her, so our relationship has had a unique dynamic. I guess it's time for me to adjust according to the fact that she seems to need me as a friend now more than she needs me as a guardian.

"You're right," I say to which a big smile spreads across her face in response.

"Okay," she says. "Then tell me everything."

When I finish telling her about Luc, leaving out any mention of sex because I am certainly not there yet, all she can say is, "A private jet? Seriously?" over and over.

"I promise you, Jules, in a dating pool like New York, a private jet is less of a rare find than him not having a huge stick up his, uh, butt.”

“You can say ass.”

“*Butt*.” I squeeze her leg. “What about you? Any lucky people fortunate enough to be crushed on by you?”

“Of course, I have crushes. I’m sixteen for Pete’s sake, but almost none of them are actual people I would ever in a million years meet. Like, I think I have a crush on half the guys I follow on TikTok and they’re complete strangers.”

“*Almost* none of them, ” I repeat her words back to her.

“Alright, sister time over,” she announces while getting up.

“Oh, come on!” I whine. Now it’s my turn to throw a pillow at her. “I told you mine.”

“Nope,” she says. “*Yours* takes you on private jets. *Mine* doesn’t know I exist. Plus, I actually promised Mom I would help her set up an Instagram account tonight.”

“One- there is no way he doesn’t know you exist and I’ll get it out of you, eventually. Two- don’t miss this opportunity to give mom a hilarious username. If you want to be treated like an adult, you gotta play with the big dogs. You got this. Make me proud.”

“You’re ruthless! See you tomorrow for dinner?”

I nod and wave her off, and as soon as I’m alone, I pick up my guitar.

My alone time doesn’t last long, as the buzzer on my apartment intercom goes off.

“Who is it?” I ask while pressing the button to connect me to the apartment’s front door.

“Hey Melody, it’s Lucien. Do you have time for me to come up for a bit?” His unmistakable voice comes through the speaker and my heart races. Why is he here? He sounds somber and without the mischievous slant I’ve come to associate with him. Even him using both of our whole names instead of the shortened versions is unusual. Did something happen?

"Oh," I say, unable to hide my confusion. "Okay, come on up." I buzz him in.

I run to the bathroom to check out my appearance before he gets to my front door. I'm wearing leggings and an old sweatshirt, my hair is all over the place, and the apartment is a mess from my unpacking. There is no time to address all these things, so I pick and choose. I throw my hair up in a bun and strip off my sweatshirt to throw on a white v-neck t-shirt over the black sports bra I have on. The apartment is hopeless, so Lucien will just have to accept that he is not doing the nasty with a type-A personality. It's better anyway that he figures that out sooner rather than later.

A knock comes at my apartment door, and I smooth my hair before opening it.

It's only been two days, but I feel my brain light up at the sight of him. He's dressed like he just came from the office, with blue slacks and a white dress shirt that reveals the outline of his chest and arms if you look close enough, which apparently I am. His hair is pushed back in a more polished look than he favored over his vacation in Finland, and he is clean-shaven.

"It's good to see you," I say, spreading my arm out long to signal that he's welcome to come in. After our awkward goodbye at the airport, I'm not really sure how we should greet each other. He texted me a million times yesterday (now that I've unblocked him). Even so, a part of me feels like I should let him set the pace after it literally scared him to be close to me in public at the airport.

"Yeah, thanks," he says. I get a close look at his face and it comes across as strange and wrong, just like his voice did over the intercom. His lips are in a firm line and his brown eyes look kind of like puppy eyes, but not the comforting kind. No, his eyebrows arched inward as if he just did something bad that he regrets.

I move to the couch and signal for him to sit.

"Do you want a water or anything?" I ask with increasing nervousness in my voice. It's clear that whatever he is here for can't be good.

"No, no thank you," he sighs as he sits down. "I'm sorry to just show up at your apartment like this. I just..." He runs his hand through his hair, tousling it out of its perfectly pushed back form. "I just knew I wouldn't be able to do it unless I came here straight away."

"Do what, Luc?" My voice comes out sharp and foreboding.

His eyes look directly at me, and I see them harden, the emotion draining from them.

"I can't see you anymore." His words hit me like a punch to the stomach. "I wanted to tell you in person."

I swallow hard instead of answering, because what the hell do you say to that. I can't believe just a minute ago, my heart raced hearing his voice. Just an hour ago, I raved over him like a little schoolgirl to my little sister. And just a week ago, I was safe from him. I hadn't let him into my heart yet. But he was the one who insisted I did, and now? Is this some kind of twisted game for him?

I look back at his face, hard and unflinching. No. I realize. It isn't a game. He just sees me as expendable. Something to throw away when he's done.

"Okay," I say, forcing the tears that are building on the rims of my eyes to stay put. I squeeze my hands tight, digging the nails into my palm to channel the rage that is beginning to course through me. "Well, you should leave then." I can't even look at him.

"I'm sorry, Mel," he reaches his hand out to touch me.

"*Don't.*" My body tenses up as if to scream at him to not get any closer. "Don't call me that, don't get near me, and don't give me some bullshit excuse. Just do me a favor and get the hell out of my apartment."

With my head turned down, I can see him clenching and releasing his fists instead of moving to the door. I need him to get out before I completely and totally lose it.

"Please, just leave now," I am begging.

He takes a big sigh and starts heading to the door. I get up suddenly and grab the lute, which is still packed in its case. He opens the door slowly and steps out. I drop the lute case on the hallway floor next to him and go to shut the door.

He holds his palm up to stop the door from shutting.

"Please keep the lute," he practically whispers it. "Please."

"I don't want it," I answer curtly.

He lets out a long breath. "Don't you," he pauses without completing the thought. "Could we just sit and talk about this a little more, so I can explain to you why?"

Now I finally let myself meet his eyes. They look enormous and terrified and a part of me wants to grab onto him and beg him to stay, beg him to explain, especially if it would take that pained expression off of his face. But that would be one too many times I let Lucien De la Roche get my hopes up. He wants to end this. There was nothing unclear about what he said, so nothing he could add would make it better.

"No," I finally answer. "I don't need Lucien De la Roche telling me yet again why I'm not good enough. Goodbye, Lucien." I say and I force the door closed despite his mouth opening to try to say something. I run to my room, collapse on the bed, and finally let myself cry. The hot tears come streaming down my face and I'm reminded of the last time I was crying like this. It was because of the same man.

Never again.

CHAPTER TWENTY-SEVEN
Lucien

"I have the utmost respect for you, Mrs. Mavis." I hear Cole's voice getting closer to my office door. "But, I am going to disregard your wishes in this case and barge in on him. Consider it a wellness check."

And with that, Cole is standing in my doorway with a very annoyed Barb trailing behind him with her hands on her hips.

"Do you want me to call security, Mr. De la Roche?" She asks, eyeing Cole.

"Not yet, but I'll let you know if that changes. Thanks, Barb." I say as Cole mouths, "sorry," to her before shutting the door.

"Dude, what the fuck," he says, plopping himself into the chair across from my desk. "Did you lose your phone in Finland and not get a new one? Or are you simply a huge asshole who has been ignoring me for a month?"

"I'm a huge asshole who has been ignoring you for a month," I answer. *Easy.*

"Yeah, figured. Well, get your ass up because you're taking me for a drink to apologize."

"I'm not sorry," I say while going back to the e-mail that I was in the middle of.

"Well you should be," Cole stands up. "While you're holed away doing whatever it is you're doing, the world has been turning, anyway. Brooke is going through a hard time and you're an absolute asshole for not knowing that."

Shit. Brooke had called me a few times, and I ignored it because I thought it would be to ream me out for Melody.

"Is she okay?" I say, giving him my full attention now.

"I'll give you the details over a glass of top-shelf scotch paid for by you," he shrugs.

"Fine, you opportunistic ass," I growl.

"Awe, that's sweet that you see opportunity in it," he smiles while looking back at his butt.

"Let's just get the hell out of here."

We go to a common spot of ours, a hotel lounge in Soho, and find refuge in two leather armchairs facing each other.

As promised, once I load Cole up with a pricey glass of whiskey, he explains one of the many reasons I'm an asshole. Brooke's father had a heart attack. He's home now, but it's looking like he has some larger health issues that are concerning. My heart breaks for their family and I hate myself for not being there for them. Brooke's dad is a ruthless businessman in the real estate industry, and an entrepreneur like my own father. It's how they became friends. The difference is, Brooke and her father's relationship was always much more loving than my own ever was with my father. When I would spend time at their house as a kid, I dreaded having to go home to our soulless Manhattan apartment.

I escape to the balcony and leave Brooke a message immediately. I don't blame her for not picking up, but hopefully my groveling helps. I text Barb to order a gift basket and work out a weekly time for my favorite private chef that specializes in healthy meals to go over to Brooke's dad's house. He won't be happy about giving up steaks, so hopefully this will help.

When I get back, Cole and I exchange childhood memories of Brooke's dad. We can't stop laughing about one memory in particular when he was banging on Brooke's door like a madman because he knew Cole was at the house and her door was locked. Before we could let him in he picked the lock, thinking he was about to discover his daughter breaking the rule of no boys alone with her in her room. Instead, he found me helping to zip Cole into one of Brooke's dresses. She had let us raid her closet for Halloween and, of course, Cole insisted on going as Samantha from Sex and the City. Brooke wasn't even home. He stuttered a nervous apology and then proceeded to compliment Cole profusely on his outfit before we left.

Before we can get lost in another story, two young women walk up to our table. They are both long and leggy and their short, tight dresses show that they are very aware of it.

"You guys mind if we join?" the girl with blonde hair tied up in a bun asks us. "It's my friend's first night in New York and I promised her we would find her some cosmopolitan men to go along with this cosmopolitan city. Lacy here is from the country and you guys certainly look like you're from the city."

I don't bother to respond but instead look at Cole, who usually is great at being a cock-block when it's girls that are interested. And while I can't say the same for all instances in the past, tonight I'm totally fine with it.

Cole looks at me and gets the memo. "Unless you've got a big ol' dick hiding under that dress, I'm not interested and my friend here only is into smashing girls' hearts so I would stay away," Cole says in a way that is meant to be dismissively, but I can see it makes the brunette girl only eye me more intensely, as if breaking her heart is exactly the quality she's looking for in a man. Sure, it's all fun and games until the slumped shoulders and quivering lip of a broken-hearted girl are seared into your brain forever, keeping you up at night so you can't have at least one good night of sleep to help make the recovery from said girl even the slightest bit easier. Not that I'm referring to any specific case or anything.

The girls linger around for a second too long, but seemingly they tire of looking at my absolutely morose face and decide to move on. *Good choice.*

"There is another update on Brooke," Cole continues. "She might be a bit mad at you for what you did to Melody."

I sigh. I knew I wasn't off the hook for that.

"I don't get it," he continues. "You were happy. *Genuinely,* happy. Why fuck it up so badly?"

"I don't want to talk about it," I say darkly, clenching my jaw.

"Dude, too bad. Life is too short for me to sit around here and let you stew in some bullshit because you're toxic masculinity doesn't want to express emotions or admit your lost."

"I'm not fucking lost, Cole." I slam my drink on the table harder than I intended. "I don't want to talk about it because it makes me fucking miserable just thinking about it. Even though it's all I can think about. I was going to screw up Melody's life if I stayed in it. She's better off without me and time will pass and everyone will get that. In the meantime, just fucking leave it alone."

A long beat of silence passes between us, which is highly unusual for Cole.

"I'm not going to leave it alone." He finally says. "Fine. Tonight we won't talk about it anymore, but I will not leave it alone until you see how absolutely fucking stupid you're being. If your life isn't compatible with someone who you actually give a shit about for the first time in your life, and who clearly cares about you, then it's not the relationship that's the issue. It's your life. Because a life that isn't compatible with love is not a life I want for my best friend.

You deserve more than that. You've got an enormous heart, Luc, and you deserve to use it."

I don't like the prickling feeling at my chest and the hot rush to my cheeks.

I don't like that Cole's words are striking me so that I feel like keeling over and throwing up.

I don't like any of it one bit because if he's right, that means I made the dumbest decision of my life. And the only solution would be something I'm not sure I can survive.

A lone saxophone spreads through the lounge like a warm sip of wine on a cold night. I let the feeling creep through me, until I shut it off, remembering that I'm not the kind of person who relishes these whimsical moments anymore. I have to shut that person off to be the man I need to be.

That's when it dawns on me. I don't like the person who is barely surviving right now going by my name. I don't like this imposter of myself. And if I take control of my own life, it would certainly kill that person I'm pretending to be, the man who I need to run my empire. But it would create an opening for a man I can actually stand being. Except the cost of taking control might be greater than I can afford.

The music creeps into my veins and I let myself sit with it. The cost of not taking control, though, means losing myself.

CHAPTER TWENTY-EIGHT
Melody

I finish my third Lana Del Rey song of the night before it's time for my break. I'm at Bowie's filling in for a band who cancelled last minute. This is my first gig since I've come back from Finland, as I've told everyone that I'm using the money from Finland to take some time to write new music. The truth is, there has been just as much wallowing as there has been new music, but at least the two seem to kind of go together nicely.

I walk over to the part of the bar where Ryan is standing behind, bartending for the night. I've managed to get away with not telling him what happened with the stranger he saw me leave with the last time I was here, but my insistence for no picklebacks and my song choices are probably a bit revealing. Ryan also was making out with Cole that night and there is a very real possibility they stayed in touch based on the depths their tongues were going.

"Hey, Mel?" Ryan says while sliding me a glass of red wine. "Don't take this the wrong way but, is there any chance of you playing at least one song that is a little more... happy? I know it's only a Thursday, but I'm pretty sure I saw at least 2 people leave to call every ex they've ever had. Lord knows, I'm about to."

I give him a small smile.

"Well," I start. "I'm writing this one song I could try out. Basically, it's about this girl who I imagine is the reason I, uh, I mean the narrator of the song, was left by her... well, her lover."

Ryan just looks at me like I've lost my mind. "It sounds like another incredibly sad song."

"Oh, sorry, I should have lead with that. It's not a sad song."

Ryan's face scrunches in confusion.

"It's not, I swear. It's an *angry* song."

Ryan rolls his eyes in exasperation. "Yes, fine. Angry songs for the rest of the night would be a vast improvement if you really can't manage *one* happy song."

"Angry songs it is," I agree while looking into my wineglass.

I shouldn't be pitying myself. It's ridiculous. The world has actual problems. People are actually suffering, which was made more than apparent today when I met up with Brooke for lunch. She broke the news to me that her father had been rushed to the hospital. I only just met Brooke and don't know her father, but I could see the pain in her eyes she was trying to hold back from me. In that moment, I realized we were going to be friends for a long time and I would do whatever I could to help her get through this.

Before I had known what she was going through, I had poured my heart out about Lucien like a total asshole. When I say pour my heart out, I mean I curtly explained how he broke things off, because let's be real, I can only pour my heart out in music and I wasn't singing in the organic lunch spot she had chosen in the middle of the West Village. And thank goodness I barely went into it, because I would have been a true jerk if we had spent the entire time talking about me, only to have her reveal what's going on with her father at the end.

She explained to me a little more about Lucien's father, how domineering he is over him and how she's always secretly hoped

Lucien would learn how to break out from under him. For some reason, she seems to think this has to do with why he ended things, especially given my connection to De la Roche Records. I know it should make me feel better, but somehow it would be easier to swallow if Lucien had broken things off for some beautiful, wealthy girl who is more in his league. It would at least confirm we really aren't meant for each other.

Instead, it made this nagging feeling in me grow even bigger. It's an overwhelming emotion that we are destroying something so rare and special. The kind of thing a person can never recover fully from ruining. It would be like finding out an unknown sonata by Mozart was tucked away in a book you had thrown into a fire, forever destroying the chance for anyone to experience the music that was hiding away there.

What the hell is even going on in my head right now? Did I just compare being with Lucien to an undiscovered Mozart sonata? *Angry song time*, I remind myself. You are angry and it's time you showed all these people you're not just sad, but you are sad *and* angry, damn it. I shoot the rest of my wine down and charge back to the stage.

I begin the first notes of the song I wrote. It's honestly a bizarre song, blaming this mythical person named Angelica who doesn't exist. But in this song she does, and I get to blame her for being cooler than me, a better singer than me, more loving than me, richer than me. Basically, "Angelica" is everything I'm not. She is who I imagine Lucien is probably curled up with right now after serenading her with some damn sexy French love song.

This vision of Lucien and Angelica makes me even more angry so I channel it into my singing and for the first time tonight, I can sense the energy of the crowd. They actually seem to like this strange little venomous song.

Go be with Angelica

She's waiting for you with her perfect hair

Under her Chanel she's completely bare

Angelica knows the value of a dollar

And Angelica doesn't ask for rent from her father

Go be with Angelica

I am yelling at the crowd, but it is only hyping them up. I really hope there is no one named Angelica here. When I get to the next chorus, a few people sing along with the first "Go be with Angelica", and when I get to the second, my heart races because even more people are singing along with it. I can't believe it myself when I actually crack a smile. I've had people sing along with me hundreds of times, but never to my own writing. Actually, now that I think about it, I've never sung any of my writing to a crowd in my entire life. My life has become one big 'fuck-it' recently, and apparently it's what I needed to finally have the guts to do this. And holy crap, this feels *good*.

I finish and people in the bar are clapping excitedly for the first time tonight. I look over to Ryan who is nodding his head in approval, as if he suddenly realized I have something in me he never knew about.

I still have about 3 more songs to go to end my set for the night. I debate testing out some of my other songs I've been working on, but they're all sad and I'm not willing to be deflated from this high by the audience disliking them. Instead, I finish up with some Amy Winehouse, Taylor Swift, and Fiona Apple because, well, lady power.

I wrap up at the bar, apologizing to Ryan for being a downer, and rush up to my apartment.

Once I get inside, I immediately set up a bench in front of my instrument wall, along with my recording equipment which has been sorely under-used lately.

It's finally time to do the thing I was beginning to think I never could. It's time I add some original music to my YouTube channel. I've been so damn afraid of being anything less than a perfect musician that I've prevented myself from even trying. But if I don't put anything imperfect out in the world, then I can never put myself out there. Because I am imperfect. I'm learning, I'm messing things up, and I'm learning all over again. And why should I be scared of that? The far scarier option is never trying at all. I'll never be an Angelica, but at least I can keep learning how to love being a Melody.

So after one raw, imperfect acoustic version of 'Angelica', I press the upload button for the whole internet to hate or love it, it doesn't really matter.

CHAPTER TWENTY-NINE
Lucien

I've made a decision that instantly has transformed my world into a completely unfamiliar place. And that's how I know the decision is the right one.

The crustiest details of Manhattan, like all the garbage stuck in the snow, suddenly look like *character* to me. The man asking me for cash on the subway is suddenly a *confident entrepreneur* in my eyes. I am seeing everything through my own, brand new perspective. And since it's solely mine to experience, I instantly like everything in this world a lot more.

And sure, that means I am like a naïve little baby pacing around in an expensive suit. Sure, that means I am going to learn things the hard way, like narrowly avoiding a broken bottle hidden in the snow. But it is all *mine* to learn. I will no longer live my life under the obsessive gaze of my father, and that means the world around me is mine for the very first time.

Feeling bolstered in my determination, I've found my way to my father's apartment already, not wanting to waste another second. Even this penthouse looks different to me. The cold, smooth interior filled with marble and chrome used to give me anxiety. It was a testament to the fact that I would never be as big as him because I could never afford an apartment like this. Sure, I can afford some of the finest apartments in the world, but it didn't matter because it would still always be a step below him and purchased with money that he was the seed for. Now, as I barge through his hall, I can feel nothing but gratitude. Because if I ever do have as much money as him, it will never be spent on an empty shell of an existence like this one. In fact, I pity him. There's not one thing of sentimental value displayed in this entire apartment, and that is really sad. But it will *never* be my future. I'm making sure of that.

I finally get to the kitchen where he and his latest blonde arm candy are sitting at a glass table, surrounded by windows showing the skyline. A chef is preparing their meal at the large onyx kitchen island.

"Lucien, now is not really a good time," he says with a wink and a lascivious smile that I've seen way too many times. I feel an ache of pain for the woman he's with, knowing how little he respects her just by the simple expression on his face. He's wordlessly bragging to his son that he's too busy hooking in a woman for the night who he'll never call again. Why would he think that's something I'm impressed and not nauseated by? I realize it doesn't actually matter to him, he doesn't care what I think.

"Well, it's the only time for me, so that's too bad for you," I walk over to the woman and extend my hand. She's about my age, which means about 30 years younger than my father. I feel her gaze burn into me, sizing me up. "Luc," I offer.

"Erica," she says with a smile.

"Erica, let me just save you some time. This man only has the capability to see you as a commodity. He'll invest in you early on, get what he wants, and then discard you. You're better off spending your time anywhere but here tonight, I can assure you."

"Oh," she says looking at my father who's greedy smile is now wiped from his face. He's not necessarily angry, more bored and slightly confused. Probably because I haven't rebelled in a long time. I quickly learned not to when I was younger, because his disinterested reaction only ended up hurting me more than anything he could have said back to me.

But this isn't just a rebellion, this is a goodbye.

When my father doesn't provide a rebuttal to my accusation, the woman stands. "I think I'll be going then," and glides off in her towering heels.

"What's this really about, Lucien?" He takes a sip of his wine.

"I'm stepping down as CEO and selling my shares in De la Roche Records to start my own media company," I say without hesitating. I have no desire to hide my intentions.

"Hah!" He laughs a cynical and cutting laugh. "That's cute. Really. Little man thinks he can drive the car just because his father bought him a toy Maserati."

"I'm not asking for your opinion, I'm only telling you so you have the option to buy my shares from me before I offer them to the board and then to the public. It seems like the right thing to do since you gave them to me."

"The right thing to do is to fulfill your obligation to our legacy," he stands now. I can see anger pulsing in the vein on his temple. I think this is the most emotion he's ever shown toward me.

"That's all I've ever been to you," I take a step closer. "Marie was always jealous of me because I got more of your attention, but really you were just investing in me so I could fulfill this duty. You never saw me as anything more than a tool for you to use." I take a deep breath. "And I see the misfortune in my shares of the company possibly going to strangers, I really do. But do you know what's even more misfortunate? My entire life, my entire personhood, and my entire soul being forfeited like a pawn because I never had the guts to get off your chessboard. I'm my own man and I will make my own legacy. I've never felt better about any decision before in my life."

I watch his eyes crest into a sickening smile. "Then I will enjoy watching you fail."

"By stepping out from under you, I've *already won*," I say and turn my back to him, walking out.

When I finally get down the elevator and outside, I take a deep breath to steady myself, but instead begin laughing. I laugh so hard I can barely breathe. I laugh like a man who has been given his life back. I laugh because it was always *this* easy, and I never saw it. I laugh and laugh until finally I collect myself, and begin to walk the 40 blocks downtown to my apartment. The cold is already stinging my face and my dress shoes aren't cut out for this kind of trek, but none of that matters because the peace that washes over me is potent enough to get me through any challenge coming my way.

This is only the beginning of a long road. I still have shares to sell, a company to create, and a girl to win back. Yet, for the first time in my life, I'm finally on the right road and I will put every single part of me into making the journey.

CHAPTER THIRTY
Melody

I'm woken up from a very comforting dream about Danny DeVito by my phone vibrating on the floor next to my bed. Panic grips my throat when I immediately realize it must be very early in the morning as the sun isn't even up. No one who knows me would call me this early unless it is an emergency.

I snatch my phone and sigh in relief. Correction- no one would call this early unless it was an emergency or they are in a ridiculously distant time zone. A picture of Lumi's face lights up my phone.

"Good morning," I say, cracking through the sleep in my voice.

"You made me famous!" She yells.

"I'm sorry," I say instinctively from being yelled at and still rubbing the sleep from my eyes. "Wait, what?"

"What? Don't apologize! Wait, what time is it there. Oh, crap. I definitely woke you, didn't I? I just got a break for lunch and had to call. You've got to check your phone."

"Hold on, I'm putting you on speaker."

I look at my phone and see it's 6:15 AM. I've set my phone to basically no notifications so I pull up each app, but sure enough there are thousands and thousands of new followers and engagements on all of them.

"How the hell did this happen?"

"That song, 'Angelica', which is absolutely epic by the way, blew up because, well, you basically described every girl imagining their ex moving on. But yeah, then people picked up on our New Year's performance of 'You Sexy Thing' from your account and now I have a ton of followers too. Melody, how can I ever thank you?"

"Just get your butt to New York City," I answer, walking to the kitchen to brew coffee.

"Deal," Lumi agrees.

We hang up and I sit, dumbstruck, listening to the drips of my coffee brewing. What the *hell* do I do now? This kind of attention is all I ever thought I needed to feel good about myself, but when I finally posted it last night, it wasn't about wanting praise. It was about making a promise to myself that I would be a little more vulnerable. But I didn't expect to feel *this* vulnerable and *this* fast.

And I know the last person I should think about is Lucien, but of course I'm thinking about him. I want to call him and tell him about it, because my gut, the part of me I've been trying to shove so deep down that I forget about it, knows he woke something up inside me that made me realize being vulnerable might be worth it. It's probably a delusional thought, as being vulnerable with him has left me in nothing but pain for the last month. Yet, I still wouldn't take any of our time together back if I have the choice.

I get up suddenly and rush to the backpack I had with me on the plane ride back with him. I haven't been able to bring myself to take out my notebook with all my stupid notes and lyrics about falling in love with Lucien and even debated throwing it onto the New York City streets with the trash. But there it is, patiently waiting for me with my favorite green pen tucked into the spine.

I open up to the song I was working on last in the notebook, the song for him. My heart physically aches rereading the words. Sure, it aches over how naïve I was, but also at how much I *felt*.

My breath stops when I notice another handwriting beneath my own.

Music needs a Melody

What is this? I didn't write this? I read on.

And she's the perfect one

Her voice is my favorite sound

And the song has just begun

I take a deep breath, trying to subdue the fire dancing across my cheeks and the watering in my eyes. Lucien must have written this while I was sleeping. The rush of him comes back to me and, for a second, it feels so good to just think about him without the lens of anger. To imagine him writing this while I sleep next to him. And I'm reminded of the reason this has been so painful, because in my deepest instinct I know what we had was real and so much of this pain is because I truly miss him. I miss the man who could complete my lyrics.

Yet, why hadn't I given him a chance to explain?

Because I couldn't handle hearing him giving me the wrong reason. I couldn't handle another rejection.

Except I should have made him tell me, and maybe we could have worked it out. I should have at least *listened*.

I get an urge to call him, but I jump in surprise when I hear the buzzer for my apartment go off. I look at my phone for a missed call, but there isn't anything. I warily go over to the buzzer and press the intercom.

"Hello?"

"Uh, hi. I saw your light was on. Melody, can I come up? I need to talk to you."

Lucien. He saw my light go on? What was he doing, waiting outside?

"Uh," I take a deep breath, rendered temporarily speechless. "Yeah, okay," I finally say with hesitance. I buzz him up and crack the door for him to come through while I pour a cup of coffee, despite my adrenaline now pumping.

His long frame peeks around the edge of the door warily and relaxes when he sees me at the table. He's wearing black sports pants and a blue crewneck sweatshirt and looks completely exhausted, but even that can't stop him from taking my breath away. After not seeing him for so long, the sight of him hits me hard and with no mercy.

"Melody," he charges toward me. I sit at the table and gesture at him to sit down with me. I don't want this to end like it did last time. I want to hear whatever he has to say.

He sits down, watching me as he does. "I was outside just waiting, unsure what the hell to do, then I saw your lights go on and I just needed to talk to you right away."

"Why now?" I ask, genuinely confused. The timing is weird considering my video went up last night.

"Because I had this big plan for what I felt I needed to do to try to make it up to you, to try to win you back." My heart races with his words. *Win me back?*

"But then of course you go and get famous overnight, and sleep through it by the way." A small smile dances across his lips when he says that, but his face grows serious again quickly. "But I couldn't sleep. I've been up all night debating what to do because I didn't want you to think I only created my plan *after* you blew up online."

"Plan?" I sip my coffee to hide my smile. I don't *want* to be smiling, but he looks so frazzled and I can't help but find it adorable.

"Yeah, I well… I bought this…" I stop him right there. I don't want any of this to be tainted by something he bought me or something he is giving me.

"Luc, stop," I say. "I'm glad you came here. I was actually thinking about you before you buzzed in."

His face softens at these words. I continue.

"I should have let you explain why you wanted to end things. Whatever it was would still hurt like hell, but I should have at least learned why."

"Melody," he places his hand over my hand and my blood quickens at his touch. "I was so fucking dumb." He takes a long breath before he speaks again. "My father made it clear that dating you was a perfect strategic move to get the heat off of De la Roche Records for canceling all those contracts. He thought if everyone could point to you as having forgiven the company, it would discourage lawsuits from the others."

I let his words sink in. The idea infuriates me, using my weakest moment for their corporate gain. But I also notice that my body doesn't have the same gut reaction of humiliation to him mentioning me being cut from my record deal.

He continues with his eyes glued to mine. "I didn't want you to be used and dragged through my shit like that and I figured there was no other option if we were dating. I was the CEO of De la Roche Records and people would pick up on you being my girlfriend in no time."

It sinks it what he is saying. "*Was* the CEO?"

He nods, a small smile breaking at the corner of his eyes. "I thought there was no way for me to live without my father's company, but I realized I had it all wrong. I actually couldn't live as the man I had to be to run that company. I couldn't live without being able to be with the one woman I want to be with. You, Mel. I resigned and am starting my own company. Which brings me to…"

"Luc," I interrupt him again. I can't hold it in any longer. "I'm sorry. I'm sorry I doubted you and didn't even let you tell me what was going on. I was just so afraid of what you would say." My voice comes out gravelly and disturbed. I feel like such an asshole, because I know immediately in my heart that what he's saying is true. This fits with who I think Luc is, who I feel he is. I painted this detailed, fantastical story about him not choosing me for a million terrible reasons, but really it was one somewhat understandable, if even a little stupid, reason. He was trying to protect me. And this whole time he's been going through it alone, when I should have been by his side.

"No, Mel, I'm sorry," his voice matches mine.

"I'm sorry," I say with a small smile.

"I'm damn sorry," he pushes his chair out and stands facing me.

"I'm so damn sorry," I push my chair out to match him.

He steps in closer to me, taking my face in his hand. "I'm so damn fucking sorry," he whispers.

I bring my hand to his face, tracing his stubbled jaw. And I have no more 'sorry' left in me, only the ability to bring my lips to his.

I tilt my head up and take his soft lips into my own. The scent that I've tried so hard to forget makes me go dizzy from the pleasure of it filling me up. His kiss is gentle and comforting and I've missed it so much. I can finally admit to myself just how much I've missed this man.

He brings his head back.

"Mel, let me show you my plan to get you back."

"Luc," I laugh. "You already got me back."

"I did?"

"Well, yeah. I mean, of course we should take it slow."

"Oh," he looks disappointed.

"You don't want to take it slow?"

"Well, when you see what I was planning, it's not exactly *slow*."

"Okay, okay, you win. You can show me what you planned. Let me get changed."

A big grin spreads across his face and I come up short trying to imagine what on earth kind of plan could make him smile that big.

When I'm ready to go, I let him take my hand and lead me out the door.

"Oh, and Mel?" He says looking back at me before he opens the door out of my apartment. "Who the hell is Angelica?"

CHAPTER THIRTY-ONE
Lucien

With Melody finally near me again, all I want to do is strip down and hold her skin to skin, as close as two humans can possibly get. But I need to show her one last thing before I let myself do that. I need to make sure she knows what she means to me.

We are bundled up against the icy February wind, walking along her street. Where we are going, we don't need a driver.

After a few blocks, we reach an old brick building that about one hundred years ago was a fabric factory. They decommissioned it and sold it to New York City Sanitation Department who uses it as storage. But not for long. It's up for sale and I happen to be the number one party in line to purchase it. The realtor agreed to give me access today, hoping to finalize the sale. And I hope he sells it to me, too. Because if he does, that means Melody said yes.

Melody's face is crumpled in confusion as I unlock the enormous iron door.

"I've always wondered what's in this building," she says as we step in.

Right now it is filled with traffic cones, city road signs, and sandbags, but the space stretches out across the entire block. It is a huge industrial space and it might be hard to visualize the potential with the light barely getting through the milky windows, but I see our future unravel before my eyes in this very space.

I take Melody's hand and pull her through the maze of city equipment until we reach an opening where I arranged a little set-up to represent my hopes and dreams for us. Before us is an electric guitar, custom pink to match her hair, and a sign that reads, "The Devil's Melody Media Co.".

I look to Melody, who's blue eyes have gone big trying to make sense of the situation I've led her into.

"Mel," I start. "You don't have to agree to anything yet if you don't want, but this space is for sale and I want to buy it. I want to start a media company here, with you. I want you to have your own recording studio here."

Before I can go on, she takes a deep breath like she has something to say. She looks slightly agitated. Not exactly what I was hoping for.

"What's wrong?" I ask when she doesn't start.

"I don't want you to think you have to buy me things. I just want you."

This makes me smile. I take her hand.

"I don't want to do this because I think it will win you back. I am doing this because you're so damn talented and I would be lucky to have you alongside me in this. Even, hypothetically, if you were someone I wasn't completely in love with, I would still believe in your talent. I want to support your skill and passion in any way possible because I think it will change the world." I take a deep breath. I've practiced this so many times, but adrenaline is coursing through me and I can't be sure I'm making sense. "And sure, fine, also because I want all of your dreams to come true and will do anything to make that happen."

Her mouth hangs open, her pink lips slack. I push my free hand through my hair nervously.

"We can change the name, of course, it's only one idea," I add.

"Luc," she starts. I warm at her choosing to call me by my shortened name. I've learned that even 'Lucifer' is a warmer nickname than the cold, formal way she uses my full name. I watch her, trying to read what she's about to say. Her eyes are big and I see that there are tears clinging to the rims of her eyes and threatening to drop any second.

I take her hand in mine. "Are you okay?"

She nods enthusiastically 'yes', and this is all it takes for her tears to run down her cheeks.

"I'm," she finally speaks in between quick breaths. "I'm just… really happy." She takes another deep breath. "And I have a break-up album that's already ready to be recorded."

I let out a deep laugh, a mix of joy and relief before grabbing her face in my hands. I use my thumb to wipe away a stream of tears running down her cheek.

"We have so much to look forward to, Mel. We're only at the beginning."

"You mean, 'the song has just begun'?" She cocks her eyebrow at me with a smile, quoting the lyrics I wrote for her in her notebook.

"Ah, you found that, huh?"

She nods. "Right before you got here this morning. I love it."

"I love you," I say it without thinking, but as soon as it comes out, it feels right. I already want to shout it again so it echoes off this high ceiling and brick walls.

Her eyes look at me with surprise, yet again. I wonder if I'll ever see her face make this expression so many times in one day again in my life. In that moment, I make a vow to myself that I will. On our anniversary, no fuck that, on random Tuesdays, I'll sweep her off her feet so I can get this reaction over and over again. I wonder if

I'll still be able to get the same rise out of her when we're 90 years old and she expects every one of my antics.

Her surprised face transforms into a big, wide smile. "I love you, Luc. Now if you don't start kissing me in the next second then I…"

Before she can finish that threat, I bring my lips to hers, hungry and giving. Her fervor matches mine, our bodies pressed against each other.

"I've missed…" I say as I gasp for air to go in for my next kiss.

"You…" She pulls at my waist, begging me to, somehow, get closer to her.

"So damn…" I breathe and grab her by her thighs, lifting her body up to straddle mine. I pin her against the brick wall and pull back to admire her.

"So damn much."

She brings her hand up to my jaw and holds her eyes to mine. "Show me how much," she whispers.

"That's going to take at least 80 years," I nudge her nose with mine.

"Well, then you better get started."

And I do.

I kiss down her neck so I can breathe in as much of her as possible. Yet apparently for Mel, this is too slow. She reaches down through all our winter layers and finds the waistband of my pants and boxers and pushes them down with urgency. I assist her in finishing the job. It's too cold in here to undress completely, but there is a way to warm up.

I place her on her feet to strip her jeans off before taking her back up around me as soon as I am done. We are moving desperately now, every second passed is agonizing.

I'm already so hard for her and my thickness pushes into the crevice forming in her light pink panties.

She reaches down between her legs and moves the lace to the

side, and I groan in approval.

"Please, Luc," she grips the hair on the back of my head and pushes my mouth to hers desperately before breaking away. "Don't make me wait any longer."

And I can't. I line myself up to her and push once and then again to take her completely up against the wall. I push deeper and she flexes over me. With this, there is nothing delicate left between us, only pure lust and need. It is not gentle, and it is not gradual. It is all of me and all of her in this moment, and we are holding nothing back from each other.

She claws at my back and I pull her thighs tighter around my waist. I bite her bottom lip with a ferocious need to possess her, like I can't get enough. She licks my teeth and my top lip with primal hunger.

I move my hands to her perfect ass and pump her up and down onto me in quicker motions. She clenches around me as her breath quickens in my ear. I have a sudden need to finish with her, just so we can start this all over again. But not until I know she is going to come so hard that she sees the damn northern lights above us in the warehouse in Brooklyn.

I drop her to the ground and fall to my knees, ripping down her soaked panties. I grab her hips and bury my face between her legs and lick her maniacally. There is no grace or teasing in my movements, only the singular focus of making her lose her mind.

When her legs begin to shake and she can barely stand, I scoop her back up and drive deep into her.

She is calling my name and I am calling hers as she trembles around me, writhing in bliss. It's all I need to lose it. I pump into her so deep that my hips alone are pinning her to the wall. The climax hits me hard and fast. I close my eyes and hold on to Mel's hands for dear life, feeling like I am being swept away in this moment.

When I finally come back to earth, I open my eyes and Mel is right there with me. The joy in her eyes might be the only thing in the world that could match the ecstasy that I feel. It hits me that this is my life now, and it's already better than it could have ever been without her.

CHAPTER THIRTY-TWO
Melody

3 Months Later

"Hm," Lumi squints her eyes at the dress I'm holding up. "Do you have anything fancier?"

She flew in two days ago and has been crashing on my couch, where she is sprawled out right now 'yaying' or 'naying' as I try to help her find something to wear. We've fallen quickly into a pattern similar to the one we had in Finland, but this time she's actually my roommate. At least for a week. Of course, I miss sharing Luc's warm bed, but for Lumi I am more than willing to make the sacrifice.

"Fancier than this?" I'm helping her get dressed for the official opening tonight of Devil's Melody Media. The dress I'm holding up is the fanciest dress I own, but it's still apparently not bold enough for her.

"No, of course she doesn't," Julia chimes in from the floor where she is going through the invite list on my computer to see who is coming tonight. I might have invited a few TikTok stars that she follows and may or may not have crushes on. Oh, and the neighborhood boy that she blushes around every time we run into him.

"I might!" Brooke strides in from my bedroom where she was getting changed. "I brought extras so you guys could help me choose what looks best." She turns around, showing us her silk champagne strap dress. She looks effortlessly stunning, as always. "What do you think?"

"Brooke, it's perfect." I say.

"Gorgeous!" Lumi chimes in.

"Woah," Julia says in awe.

Eventually, after some wardrobe shuffling, I settle on a white wrap dress that belongs to Brooke. Lumi ends up wearing my blue dress that Julia stitched stars on that I wore on New Year's Eve. And Julia is wearing her own creation- a pink peasant dress that matches her pink converse sneakers. The weather is showing hints of the impending summer and it's finally warm enough to not wear tights or big coats, so not much time passes before we are finally ready to walk the few short blocks to my future.

Just as I finish double-checking that I have everything, a knock comes at the door. I look at the girls, confused, before I open it up.

On the other side is Luc, staring at me with his devilish grin. He looks absolutely dapper in his grey-blue suit and a white shirt unbuttoned one button at the top. Standing behind him are my parents with big smiles on their face. Especially my mom, who literally glows anytime Luc is around.

"You look absolutely stunning," he says while pulling me into his arms. "I'm here to pick you up for our date."

I laugh, remembering when he came to my hotel room on New Year's Eve in Finland, just to walk me to my performance. His charm has only grown since those early days and here I am, in his arms, utterly succumbed by it.

Apparently, Luc picked my parents up for our "date" as well. He explains he thought it would be nice if we all walked over together.

He is right. We all chatter happily on the short walk to our new headquarters. The spring air and the sun peaking over the buildings create this a sensation of euphoria all around us, promising us a fresh start. It couldn't be a more perfect day for it.

The party is better than I could ever have expected. Everyone seems to have brought that excited energy of spring. The entire room is buzzing with positivity and celebration and when I look around, I see so many people from our worlds brought together. My parents are chatting with Brooke. Lumi and my sister are as thick as thieves, scouring the event for celebrities. And even Cole and Ryan have reunited, not making out this time, but laughing at something near the bar.

We hired a band that I've heard preforming in the subway to play for the evening. They're elevating the energy of the room with their brass instruments, covering an impressive variety of songs.

I'm chatting with a musician who Luc cut at De la Roche Records, but I insisted we bring to DM Media. He's a young man who is the first generation living in the U.S., with his parents from El Salvador. He mixes the traditional music of his heritage with R&B sounds. I have been absolutely addicted to his songs, listening to them all week. While I'm talking to him, I think to myself how I can't believe this is my reality now. I get to just spend my life absorbed in music, both my own and others'.

Suddenly, I notice the band is taking quite a long time starting their next song, so I look to the stage. To my surprise, it's no longer the band standing there, but Luc. He's plugging in an electric bass guitar and a man who looks familiar, but I can't quite place, is standing in front of the other microphone with his own electric guitar.

Finally, Luc straightens up and scans the crowd until he finds me and smiles. We have already given our welcoming speeches to the guests, so I don't know what this is about.

"I want to dedicate this song to 11-year old Melody," Luc starts in his microphone, "and to my friend Ted here, who planted a seed in Melody that blossomed into the beautiful gift she has today." Luc smiles ear to ear while he looks at me before turning his head down to his guitar. My heart races. It's Ted, my first ever music teacher. I've constantly wondered how he is doing and if I would ever be able to thank him. And here he is. Luc must have tracked him down.

I'm trying to hold my tears back when I feel a tap on my shoulder. It's a beautiful redhead woman, maybe in her 40s, with a tween looking boy and slightly younger girl, each tucked under one of her arms. I don't recognize any of them.

"Hi, I'm Elle," she says with a broad smile while outstretching her hand. "I'm Ted's wife and these are our kids."

I squeal in delight and introduce myself, making sure to tell them how much Ted changed my life when I was about the kids' age. We quiet down to listen to Luc and Ted's rendition of "Aerials", the same song I performed for my talent show.

I watch in awe, seeing a part of my past thrown into the middle of my present and future. It helps me to see my life so much more clearly. I think how my hardest moments allowed for a beautiful light to become visible, like the auroras breaking through on the darkest and coldest days of winter in the arctic. I feel like that 11-year-old little girl suddenly, but this time I'm finally able to witness the beauty of my life unfolding before me. Tears finally break free, away from my eyes and down the crest of my smile.

After Luc and Ted finish, they join Elle and I, giving me the chance to thank these two men profusely, over and over again. I offer for their kids to come in and do some recording sessions here for fun, because of course he is raising them as musicians.

The night devolves into a big jam session. Lumi takes the stage at one point, transfixing every eye on her during her rendition of

"Blank Space". The girl is a natural star. A few of the artists we've already signed play their music. Even Ted gets up again to play some Metallica and the awe in his children's eyes makes me smile.

When there is a lull, I decide it's finally my turn.

I walk up there with my pink electric guitar, which I leave at my studio here. Even though I've begun recording a lot of my angry break-up songs, and 'Angelica' has continued in its popularity, none of these are the songs that feel right tonight. Instead, I take out my notebook and set up for one of the most precious songs I've ever written. It's the first love song I ever wrote for the first and last true love I've ever experienced.

I begin to sing the first verse while looking to Luc. To my surprise, he navigates through the crowd and comes up with me on stage, grabbing his bass guitar. He joins, strumming along, and when it gets to the chorus, he sings the lyrics that he wrote on the plane when I was sleeping.

I smile at him, loving how every word comes dripping out of his mouth. When it's time for the next verse, I sing my own lyrics that I've added only recently.

Did they sound hollow?

Every love song

Sang before you

Can you hear it now?

My voice shakes

In awe that you're true

The I finish with my version of the chorus I wrote on the place. But when I look to Luc and notice his face is no longer smiling. In fact, he seems to look a little scared? It could be because he hasn't written another closing verse to the song. I try to look at him to signal that it's okay, that I can sing something I wrote instead. Yet, when it comes time, he does start singing.

Having you everyday

Is my own

Personal miracle

My Melody,

Will you say yes to,

This for forever?

Luc stops strumming and we lock eyes, but before I can process what is happening he is already down on one knee. He pulls out a deep blue velvet box. He flips it open to reveal a shining art-deco diamond ring. I look to him in utter shock. Am I dreaming right now?

"Will you marry me, Melody Greco?" Luc's voice shakes.

I don't know why, but the only thing my body can do is fall down onto my knees to embrace him in a hug before locking my lips with his. We separate to look at each other and we both begin laughing in delirious joy. I notice people in the background cheering and clapping.

"Yes!" I say when I realize I should actually answer. "Of course!"

Luc lifts me up to my feet along with him.

"I had this whole thing planned for when everyone left, but when I was singing, it just felt right," he whispers, using his thumb to brush away some of my tears.

"It is right," I pull him in for another kiss. "Luc, with or without a ring, I know your my eternity."

He pulls my body into his, embracing me in an all-encompassing hug. He bring his lips down to my ears. "See? I told you it was a happy ending," he whispers, warming my heart even more.

I look up at him and shake my head. "No, my love, this is only the happy beginning."

And it's true. The song of us has only just begun.

And I can't wait to hear the rest.

EPILOGUE

Lucien

2 Years Later

"Oh!" One of our nurses exclaims as another nurse whispers to her through the door.

I look from them back to Mel who is laying in the hospital bed. She looks ethereal with her flushed cheeks and sweat-lined skin. It's the most beautiful sight I've ever witnessed- the love of my life on the brink of bringing another life into this world. I squeeze her hand, reminding her I'm right here.

The nurse closes the door and looks to us. Excitement brims her face. "You won! You won Best Album of the Year!" She finally exclaims.

"Oh, my..." Mel exclaims, her eyes go big before suddenly transforming into a grimace. "Argh!" She shouts instead of finishing that sentiment. Her body heaves, her eyes clasp shut, and her nails dig into my arm. Tears run down her face and I don't know if they're from joy or pain, but it's safe to assume it's probably both.

"Something's happening!" Mel exclaims. Both terror and

excitement line her eyes as she looks up to me.

"Something's happening!" I repeat because I don't know what else to do.

The nurses swarm around her and I give them their space, reminding Mel a million times how much I love her as I do.

Two hours later, Mel has brought our little girl into the world. I stand in amazement next to them, my two girls. Our daughter is wrapped up like a little bean and asleep on Mel's chest. Mel has the most beautiful smile on her face, one I've never seen before. It radiates pure peace and joy and fills me with the same sensation.

"What about Aurora?" Mel whispers. We hadn't picked out a name because we were waiting to find out the gender. And a part of me wanted to meet our little one before choosing.

I gaze at our daughter, her little hands and her perfect little eyelashes. She is a miracle of nature, like a sky full of glowing colors, and like the weekend Mel and I reunited in Finland.

"It's the perfect name," I agree before bending down to give not one, but two, of my girls kisses. Aurora's pink eyelids flutter slightly at my touch before shutting again.

"Luc?" Mel's eyes twist suddenly in confusion. "Did I hallucinate or did the nurse say we won Best Album at the Grammy's?"

I let out a roaring laugh and Aurora's eyes flutter again at my disturbance. You'll get used to it, I wish I could tell her, our house is full of all kinds of noises.

"You won, my love," I tell her. "In one night, you brought our daughter into this world and became a Grammy winner."

She brings her hand to mine and laces her fingers through it. "We did that."

Mel looks to me and back to Aurora, and then back to me. "How did we get so lucky?"

"I wake up and wonder that every day," I answer, squeezing her hand.

"Oh yeah," she cocks her eyebrow. "Any luck on finding an answer?"

"Well, I do have one theory…"

She adjusts herself, as if settling in to be told a long story. "Well, go ahead."

"Okay, hear me out… When we walked into that cafe in Finland, we didn't know it then, but we were actually entering a witch's home."

"Anja?!" Mel says, her face aghast.

"Yep, Anja was a witch. But not an evil witch, or necessarily a good witch, just a woman with magical powers. And our fate was in her hands when we walked in, but…"

"What? What happened?" Mel asks impatiently when I pause.

"Then, you spoke your perfect Finnish when you ordered because you have a big heart and made sure to learn a language so you could connect with everyone. And this made her decide to curse us… or bless us? What's the word for a good curse?"

Mel shrugs.

"Okay, well, she cast a spell over us, giving us everything we ever wanted. So, who can Aurora and I thank for all this, including us being together?"

"Lumi for teaching me Finnish?"

I shake my head. "You, Mel. This life is all because of you. Spell or no spell."

She eyes me, smiling at my version of events, albeit a bit skeptically.

"Well, Aurora and I happen to think you might have had something to do with it."

My girls. Teaming up against me already. I give them both another round of kisses, unwilling to fight so early in my relationship with my daughter.

We spend the rest of the evening on video calls with all the people who we want to celebrate this momentous day with. We introduce Aurora to her Aunt Brooke, Aunt Lumi, Aunt Julia, and Uncle Cole. She certainly has a lot of strong ladies as role models in her life. My mother and my sister call when they wake up to the news in France, and Mel's parents promise to visit us tomorrow morning.

The evening is so full of love, from both our friends and strangers who love the music that Mel is putting out into the world. It feels as though this tidal wave of affection has come on suddenly, but the truth is, we've gradually built up to this for the past two years.

I think back to the cold and lonely month when I assumed my life was destined to be one big empty void out of my control. Changing my life seemed too reckless to even contemplate, but it turns out the only reckless thing would have been to continue on my path without change. I would have been a miserable man who would only make the lives of other's miserable, too.

Yet, Mel showed me there was something worth taking control for and, for that, I am grateful every single day.

And now we get to let our daughter shape her own life. Well, for the most part, because let's face it, she has no other choice but to be a musician.

As if on cue, she lets out the smallest little squeak.

"She's learning to sing," I say to Mel, who smiles at Aurora dreamily and then up at me.

She takes my hand and whispers.

"Our new favorite song."

Thank you for reading *A Love Song for Lucifer*.

Want more?

Sign up for the newsletter to get fun bonuses like…

+ The full lyrics for Melody's songs, "Angelica" and "Love Song for Lucifer".

+ Updates on when Brooke and Lumi get to tell their stories for the *Leading Ladies Series*.

+ Lots of other fun updates yet to be dreamed up!

Get ***Willa's Lively Updates*** here: bit.ly/33lEr4i

Or follow on:
Instagram: @willa_lively
Twitter: @willa_lively
TikTok: @willalivelyauthor